"I REALLY SHOULD BE GOING," NICOLE WHISPERED.

Rand bent his head, his lips almost brushing hers. "I guess you should," he admitted, drawing even closer.

Suddenly a loud clap of thunder broke the silence of the night. Nicole took a step back from Rand.

"That was close." Rand's voice was low.

"Yes, the lightning was very close. This could be quite a storm."

He grinned. "Count on it."

"Well, I'd better be going. I've got lots of work to do."

"There are other nice things to do on rainy nights, Nicole."

Ignoring his tempting invitation, she dashed into the downpour. "See you later!"

"You can count on that too," he whispered.

CANDLELIGHT SUPREMES

153 JEWEL OF INDIA,
Sue Gross

154 BREATHLESS TEMPTATION,
Eleanor Woods

155 A MAN TO REMEMBER,
Tate McKenna

156 DANGER IN PARADISE,
Kit Daley

157 DARK PARADISE,
Jackie Black

158 SHATTERED SECRETS,
Linda Vail

159 LIAR'S MOON,
Heather Graham

160 ESCAPE FROM THE STORM,
Barbara Andrews

161 RUNAWAY LOVER,
Alison Tyler

162 PRISONER IN HIS ARMS,
Dallas Hamlin

163 TEXAS WILDFIRE,
Eleanor Woods

164 SILVER LOVE,
Hayton Monteith

165 ADVENTURE WITH A
STRANGER,
Donna Kimel Vitek

166 LOVERS AND LIARS,
Deborah Sherwood

167 THE PERFECT EXCHANGE,
Andrea St. John

168 THE GENTLEMAN FARMER,
Lynn Patrick

A SECRET ARRANGEMENT

Linda Vail

A CANDLELIGHT SUPREME

Published by
Dell Publishing Co., Inc.
1 Dag Hammarskjold Plaza
New York, New York 10017

Dell ® TM 681510, Dell Publishing Co., Inc.

Candlelight Supreme is a trademark
of Dell Publishing Co., Inc.

Candlelight Ecstasy Romance®, 1,203,540, is a registered
trademark of Dell Publishing Co., Inc., New York, New York.

ISBN: 0-440-17672-7

Printed in the United States of America

May 1987

10 9 8 7 6 5 4 3 2 1

WFH

To Our Readers:

We are pleased and excited by your overwhelmingly positive response to our Candlelight Supremes. Unlike all the other series, the Supremes are filled with more passion, adventure, and intrigue, and are obviously the stories you like best.

In months to come we will continue to publish books by many of your favorite authors as well as the very finest work from new authors of romantic fiction. As always, we are striving to present unique, absorbing love stories —the very best love has to offer.

Breathtaking and unforgettable, Supremes follow in the great romantic tradition you've come to expect *only* from Candlelight Romances.

Your suggestions and comments are always welcome. Please let us hear from you.

Sincerely,

The Editors
Candlelight Romances
1 Dag Hammarskjold Plaza
New York, New York 10017

A SECRET
ARRANGEMENT

CHAPTER ONE

Nicole Sabine felt as if her head might explode at any moment. After three straight hours on the phone her back was stiff, her left ear sore, and her grip on reality fading fast. She pushed away from her desk and stood up, groaning softly to herself as she stretched the kinks out of protesting muscles.

"Great," Nicole muttered, limping slightly as she started down the narrow aisle between the desks lining both sides of the outer office. "Come on, foot. Wake up."

The room buzzed with activity, six different people engaged in six different telephone conversations, though all had the same tone of cajoling urgency. Nicole couldn't help eavesdropping on each as she passed.

"Of course I can get them to you by Tuesday morning but only if you order right now."

"You won't find a better price."

"All right, I'll take that much a stem but only if you take two thousand."

"I told you those freesia would be gone in an hour. How about some nice glads?"

A young man in a tan knit shirt and jeans waved Nicole over as she went by his desk, a phone receiver wedged between his ear and shoulder.

"Maybe. Let me ask the boss." He covered the receiver with his hand. "What's the status on sweetheart roses?"

Nicole paged through a sheaf of papers on his desk and pointed. "Right there, Tony."

"Oh. They're ours." His face reddened. "Sorry."

"You're doing fine. I don't expect you to know it all the first week."

"Thanks."

She smiled and continued on, sighing when yet another employee waved at her. "What's up, Sam?"

"Big order."

"Hmm," she hummed as she glanced at his scribbled note. "That'll make a nice wedding, all right." Nicole looked up at him warily. "But I don't recognize the retailer."

The man shifted uneasily. "It's the father of the bride."

"You know the rules, Sam. Retail and whole-sale florists only. No individuals."

"A sale's a sale, Nicole," he said, warning her defiantly.

"Sabine doesn't bypass retailers. Got that?"

"Yeah." He muttered something under his breath as she walked away.

Nicole stopped in her tracks. "Excuse me?"

"I said maybe I should go to work for Jameson. I'll bet he doesn't turn away orders."

"I couldn't care less what Rand Jameson does!" Nicole told him loudly and immediately regretted it. For one thing, it wasn't good for the boss to lose her cool, and for another, it made her headache worse. "He's certainly willing to cut my throat," she continued in a calmer tone, "so I wouldn't put it past him to slip into retail on the side. More power to him. Word will get around and the trade will bury him. That's why we've never done it and never will, and if you don't like it, Sam, maybe you should move on."

"Hey! I was just—"

Nicole cut him off by stepping out of the office and closing the door behind her. Down the stairs, out into the bright sunlight, through a tightly sealed door, and she instantly felt the tension draining away. Her head stopped pounding. She started to relax. Taking deep breaths of the moist, heavily scented air, she closed her eyes and sighed.

Home. Her apartment was a place where she slept, the office behind her a place where she spent most of her waking hours these days. But here in the greenhouse, chest-deep in a sea of living color, surrounded by the growing flowers that had been her life practically from birth, was home.

Her grandfather had emigrated from Europe to settle on the land beneath her feet. He and his two sons had built the wholesale flower business of which she now controlled an important part. Sabine was a respected name in the trade—top-quality cut flowers at fair prices.

It was in her blood, this business. Three generations of Sabines, their roots deep in the soil, domestic growers supplying flowers for every stage of people's lives. Nicole considered the profession just as important as farming. Wheat and vegetables were food for the body, flowers food for the soul.

Not all of the Sabines through the years had the same feelings, of course. Her grandfather had split the land some time back, half to each son, Nicole's father taking over the flowers and her uncle starting a gardening outlet and nursery. When the time was ripe, her uncle had sold his half to a developer.

But her father's greenhouses remained. Not all who worked the flowers were Sabines, but it was very much a family affair. Nicole, two sisters, a brother, a smattering of cousins, and naturally Nicole's mother and father worked in some phase of the operation. Even her grandfather could still be found puttering around on his good days. It came as no surprise to any of them that Nicole was the one who was gradually assuming the informal throne of Sabine Wholesale Flowers.

She was her grandfather's favorite, and as the patriarch would tell anyone who would listen, she was as sharp as a rose thorn. Standing out like a prize hybrid, Nicole had something the others cheerfully admitted they did not: a head for both flower growing *and* business.

In a world of high energy and labor costs, fluctuating markets and extremely competitive foreign imports, Nicole was keeping them afloat. She had to. Sabine would never sell out, and they would always be growers. But some traditions had to be broken. Nicole had only done what had to be done.

Her decisions hadn't been easy, nor popular, with the family at first, but eventually they accepted her wisdom. The competition had to be faced, and if you could import something cheaper than you could grow it, you had to swallow your pride and do just that. Simple.

"Move it or lose it!" The voice behind her was gruff and heavily accented. *"Vite! Vite!"*

Nicole's eyes popped open, and she spun around to find her grandfather, Vincent Sabine, careening down the aisle toward her, pushing a wheelbarrow full of a mixture of rich, black soil and fertilizer. He was a rough, thick-boned man, his head of unruly gray hair and bushy mustache framing clear blue eyes that sparkled with an almost maniacal intensity. She managed to jump out of his way in the nick of time as he barreled past.

"What on earth—"

"My orchids are starving!" Vincent informed her. "I could use some help, you know," he added in a tone that was meant to make his granddaughter feel guilty.

He was eighty-one and his health fluctuated, but even on his bad days Vincent Sabine was rudely strong and almost unstoppable. His retirement, if one could call it that, consisted mainly of tending his orchids, counseling any of the family wise enough to seek his advice, and terrorizing the rest. Nicole felt sorry for anyone who got in his way.

"You make it sound as if I force you to do these things," she said as she rushed after him. The uneven brick walk beneath her feet was treacherous for the uninitiated, but she had been playing in and running through this myriad array of greenhouses from the time she could walk. "We have mixing tanks and delivery systems for the finest, most carefully balanced fertilizers available, Vin. You're the one who insists on using sheep—"

"Chemicals!" He made a spitting sound. "Not for my orchids. Open the door for me, Nicole. *Vite!*"

She dashed around him as he slowed at the end of the aisle, his fragrant load tipping precariously. "Yes, Vin."

Everyone called him Vin, not because his first name was Vincent but for the *vin ordinaire* he consumed in amazing quantities. The technology he spoke of with such distaste had become a profitable necessity and he knew it, but he didn't have to like it, so he had retired to let Nicole's father run that end of things.

But Vin made his presence known. The small greenhouse he and Nicole entered was his private territory. A wall full of best-of-show ribbons divided the humid, hot, almost cloyingly sweet-scented solarium from the commercial operations, rows of outrageously healthy orchids a testimony to the foolishness of questioning his growing methods.

"Well?" he asked as he carefully began to distribute handfuls of fertilizer to the beautiful flowering plants surrounding them. "Have you forgotten how?"

Nicole scowled at him, pushed the sleeves of her pale pink silk blouse up to her elbows, and defiantly dug right in with her hands, as he was doing. Forget how, indeed!

"Just because I spend most of my time on the phone these days doesn't mean I've lost my touch, Vin."

"I know." He leaned over and kissed her on the cheek. "You are a Sabine, Nicole. You have this in your veins," he informed her seriously, grabbing a handful of black earth. "More than any of my children or their children."

They worked in happy silence for a while, Nicole glowing with the compliment. Vin watched her out of the corner of his eye. She looked like his wife had at that age: thick hair the color of sun-ripened wheat, curling under at the ends to softly frame her face; a face full of life, with high cheekbones and gray-green eyes.

Her grandmother's hands had been more graceful, with a finer bone structure, but Vin found Nicole's just as pleasing; hers were strong hands, accustomed to working with growing things. All the Sabine women had somewhat full hips and were less than generously endowed in the chest. Nicole was no different. Perhaps a bit taller than average. Not striking, perhaps, but Vin would say she was pretty, even if she weren't his granddaughter.

"You are too thin, Nicole."

"Thank you so much," she said dryly. Her grandfather and she had a very good relationship. They had been close for as long as she could remember, both equally blunt, honest, and capable of acid humor. "You are a crazy old man who likes fat women."

"I am French," he replied proudly, as if that were the only explanation necessary. "I like all women. And you are still too thin."

She shrugged. "It's the new style."

"Starvation?" He snorted derisively. "A woman should be full and round."

"Then you and your son," she informed him, "should have married women with big bosoms. Their genes have doomed me to being flat."

Vin sighed loudly. "I did not say you were flat. I said you were skinny. Look at your sisters. They have meat on their bones. Are they fat?"

"Well, no, but . . ."

16

"You see?"

Nicole glared at him. "They don't have the kind of responsibilities I have, Vin. You know what I mean."

He blinked, then grinned broadly. "This is true. Look at me," he replied, patting his rotund stomach. "You see what retirement has done to me? I used to be a rail."

"Who are you trying to fool? That's all muscle," she said, prodding his paunch playfully. "But you see what I mean. Even with Dad handling everything but the business side, running Sabine is still enough to keep one thin."

"I handled the growing and the selling by myself," Vin objected proudly, "and didn't waste away."

"With Dad's help and half the family working for you," Nicole reminded him.

"Not at first."

She smiled. They had this discussion about once a week. "The business has changed, Vin."

"I know, Nicole. I know," he admitted. "We don't just grow and sell anymore. Now we import and broker and move things we never grew from here to there. So many people in the office who never touch the soil. It's crazy."

"It works."

Vin beamed at her. "Yes. We are doing well."

"We are doing better," she said, correcting him. "Dad's still the best grower around, and I'm getting the hang of importing. Now, if Rand

Jameson would drop off the face of the earth, I'd probably gain that weight you say I need."

"Jameson," Vin agreed darkly. "It is good you run that part of things now, Nicole. Your father and I do not understand men like him. I have no sympathy for the growers who failed because they spent their time complaining instead of meeting the competition. But this new competition! He isn't a grower. What is he doing in this business?"

"What he's doing, Grandfather," she replied, "is making a lot of money. It's his right. He's a smart man who knows how to buy and sell. If we don't stay on our toes, he'll buy and sell *us* one day."

"Never!"

"He's good, Vin. And he's fast. His is a streamlined operation with lower overhead than ours. He undercuts my prices at every turn."

Her grandfather patted her hand and shrugged. If she lived to be a hundred, Nicole thought, she never would be able to shrug that expressively. The French must have invented the shrug.

"Our turn will come, Nicole. I don't know importing, but it seems we should use our size against him. Be more aggressive and trust your instincts. Beat him at his own game."

Nicole stared at him for a moment, then grinned. "You're right. Instead of keeping pace with Jameson, I should be trying to outdistance him." She looked down at her fertilizer-covered hands. "You know, Vin, I think this stuff must have finally worked its way up to my brain."

The old man exploded with laughter. "You see? I've always said I could make anything grow!"

"Not again. What's their problem this time?"

"Who can tell? You know the Colombians, Rand. The airline is owned by the government, and if the government says don't fly, they don't fly," the man on the other end of the telephone line replied.

Rand Jameson leaned back in his chair, extending his long legs and putting his feet up on the battered metal army surplus desk. One of these days he'd have to go shopping for some new office furniture. Maybe he'd even put up some partition walls, give himself a bit more privacy.

Then again, what was the point? Jameson Wholesale Floral had outgrown every building it had occupied so far, and yet another move to a larger warehouse was long overdue. Maybe this time, instead of moving the junk, he'd just have someone haul it off and furnish the new place right, with oak or walnut or teak, perhaps even real walls.

Watch the overhead, Rand, he thought to remind himself. The money would go into a larger, more efficient cooler, a new truck, more incoming and outgoing telephone lines and salesmen to work them. If anything was left over, then he could worry about sprucing up the office.

19

"Damn," he grumbled.

"Just part of the business, Rand," the importer from Miami said. "It happens to everybody."

Rand muttered a few more choice epithets. "Yeah, I know. Bogota gets ticked off, customs in Los Angeles finds a bug or two, or somebody in New York decides there's contraband on a flight and rips the plane apart while the flowers bake on the runway."

"At least it doesn't come out of our pockets. Imagine how the exporters feel when they find out they have to eat another shipment."

"I suppose." Rand brushed a lock of jet-black hair away from his hazel eyes, then pinched the bridge of his nose between a thumb and forefinger. Speaking of overhead, one couldn't forget the aspirin bill. "Imagine how I feel. I have to scramble and find another product my clients will fall in love with and decide they have to have."

"For some bizarre reason sweetheart roses are a big thing this month. But I can't help you there, buddy. Maybe California or Chicago?"

"Not for a price I can live with. I set my margin too low. If I don't have to pay freight, I might just keep my shirt, and that means a local grower."

The other man laughed uproariously. "Sabine? You'd better watch that rivalry, Rand," he informed him. "One of these days they'll stick it to you. Like maybe today."

"You're just full of cheerful observations, aren't you?"

"You'll survive."

"Count on it."

After he hung up, Rand sat looking at the phone, one finger hovering over the button that would automatically dial Sabine's number. He ordered from Sabine quite often. Everyone in Colorado did; it was an economic necessity.

Such was their rivalry, however, that they always treated him differently from the others. The moment he identified himself, he would be transferred to that sanctimonious hellcat in charge, Nicole Sabine. Lord, she'd love it if she knew how badly he needed to cut a good deal on this one.

He'd never been formally introduced to her, but he'd seen her around. It amazed him how such a wisp of a girl stubbornly had managed to keep Sabine going when most of the local growers had opted to sell their land and live off the interest. Of course, she hadn't done it alone; all the Sabines were involved in the operation, and they were all tough as nails.

It was about time he met Nicole Sabine face-to-face. Rand had done well in this business, and he knew that some of his success had been at Sabine's expense. She would hardly welcome him with a smile. Still, there was no reason their rivalry couldn't be a bit more friendly. Competition was stiff in wholesale flowers, but there was room for them both. They didn't have to claw at each other, did they?

He stood up and stretched, dismayed to find a

kink in his back. No doubt about it, he had to get more exercise. Not that he was getting fat by any means. The stomach was still as flat as a board, the muscle tone good, plenty of power in his broad shoulders and strong arms. Lots of guys let themselves go to seed in their early thirties. Not Rand.

In school he had played a lot of basketball, as most six-foot young men with sure hands and a modicum of natural agility did. After casting about for a while after graduation, looking for something different, he took a job loading trucks for a wholesaler, an occupation that kept him in shape, built up muscle, and had given him the idea for starting his own business. That had been tough, too, mentally and physically.

But he hadn't had to do much of the physical stuff for a few years now and spent more time than he liked cooped up in the office. Maybe he'd take up tennis again or join a recreational league and play some ball. He could run rings around all the saggy executives.

Or maybe, Rand thought as he climbed in his van for the trip to the rival wholesaler, maybe he could just make it a habit to confront Nicole Sabine once a week. The thought alone seemed to have his adrenaline pumping.

"One never knows," he said to himself as he drove along.

He was willing to bet that Nicole Sabine wasn't fragile. There was something about her, something rather exotic and sensual. She was certainly

22

a fierce competitor, and that attracted him too. Rand grinned broadly and started humming. Yes, indeed. He should have thought of standing face-to-face with the competition long ago.

CHAPTER TWO

"Did we order anything from Jameson?" Nicole's sister, Jean, asked, peering out the office window as she sipped at a cup of coffee.

Nicole looked up from some papers on her desk. "You're kidding, right? The only thing Rand Jameson has that I want are his accounts."

"Well, one of their vans just pulled up outside."

"Strange. I don't think we have anything for them," Nicole remarked, flipping through a stack of orders. "As a matter of fact, Mr. Jameson hasn't gotten anything from us yet this month. The Colombians must be treating him well."

Her coffee temporarily forgotten, Jean practically pressed her nose up against the window-pane. "Come look, Nicole. You won't believe this. I don't."

"What?" Glad for the break in her bookkeeping chores, Nicole joined her sister at the window. "You're right. I don't believe it. It's the devil himself."

The two women watched as Rand made his

way from the parking lot to the redbrick building that housed Sabine's offices. He slowed as he walked past row upon row of greenhouses, seemingly impressed.

"I wonder what he wants," Jean mumbled.

"We'll find out soon enough."

Rand Jameson. Nicole had seen him before, at a trade function or two. He hadn't approached her, and that had been fine with her. But he was here now, heading toward the office, presumably to talk to her.

He was rather handsome in a rough sort of way, strong-looking with broad shoulders and chest. His hair was jet-black and longish, yet carefully trimmed. The white cotton shirt he wore had short sleeves, displaying tanned arms, and was tucked into his gray slacks. Nicole could see he had no fat around his middle. He was tall, long-legged, and on his feet were expensive-looking loafers that wouldn't last a day around the Sabine operation.

She glanced down at herself. Her silk top was very nice, and her jeans were new, but the well-worn sneakers would have to go. As Jameson disappeared from view around the corner of the building, Nicole stepped over to the closet in the corner and changed into a pair of wedge-soled sandals. They went with the outfit and looked much better, in addition to giving her an extra couple of inches. She didn't want to have to look up at him.

Jean watched her with wry amusement. "Relax, Nicole. He's probably here to talk business, not play volleyball. Maybe he wants to bury the hatchet."

"In my head, I'll bet," Nicole returned sarcastically.

"Give the guy a break."

"Why? He's never given us one."

She grinned. "I think he's kind of cute."

"So is a weasel, until you see its teeth."

Through the glass partition separating Nicole's small office from the sales crew, they watched the front door and waited for Jameson to walk in.

Unaware that his arrival was being so warily anticipated, Rand paused at the foot of the stairs leading up to the offices. Was this a good idea? His drivers had been here before to pick up orders, but he'd never set foot on the place, so the Sabines were bound to be suspicious right off the bat. It was such an unprecedented move on his part that they might figure out just how badly he needed their product.

Then again, his visit would undoubtedly catch them off-guard. He would be cagey, maybe ask for a tour, and pretend that meeting Nicole Sabine was something he'd been meaning to get around to for a long time. After a bit he could casually work up to what he needed—without letting it seem like it was his real reason for being there, of course.

Rand wouldn't have to feign interest. This was quite an impressive operation. Not that he was overwhelmed. After all, they did perhaps twice the volume as his company, but he imported twice as much. They trounced him on domestics; he squashed them on exotics.

That was the root of their rivalry; Sabine had to import more to offset rising greenhouse costs, only to find that Jameson was able to cut their throats because he had been ordering and selling more of those imports all along.

"Looking for somebody?"

Rand turned and saw a young man in a tan knit shirt and blue jeans coming out of what appeared to be an employee lounge. He smelled food; it reminded him that he'd skipped lunch himself today.

"Is Nicole Sabine around?" he asked.

"I think she's upstairs," the young man replied. "Come on, I'm going up too. I'll take you to her." He bounded up the stairs with Rand close behind.

When they walked into the office, Rand felt every eye in the room upon him as he followed the employee down an aisle between two rows of desks. As he passed by him one man pointedly turned a sheaf of papers over on his desk, as if Rand were there to spy.

The young man knocked on a door at the end of the aisle. Through a glass partition at the side of the door Rand could see two women inside. One was standing there sipping coffee, looking back at him with frank appraisal. The other sat behind a solid-looking oak desk, seemingly ignoring him. Rand smiled slightly. Nicole Sabine. The door opened.

"Excuse me, Jean. There's a guy here wants to see Nicole."

"Thank you, Tony," Nicole said from her seat at the desk. Her sister stood in the doorway, still staring at Rand. Nicole cleared her throat irritably and added, "Jean, let Mr. Jameson in, please, and then help Tony go over the status reports for tomorrow."

"Jameson?" Tony asked. "Rand Jameson?"

"Come on, Tony," Jean said, stepping past Rand and taking the young man's arm. "I can see we have neglected certain areas of your training." She closed the door behind her on the way out.

Alone together in the small office now, Rand and Nicole sized each other up for a moment. Nicole noted the small smile on his face, the self-confidence in his hazel eyes, and the calm, masculine assurance of his stance. His easy manner irritated her. What was he doing here?

"What can I do for you, Mr. Jameson?" she asked, neither offering him a chair nor getting up to shake his hand.

She was tough, all right. And all business. Rand could practically feel the ice in her voice. "For a start, Ms. Sabine," Rand replied as he took a seat in one of the chrome-and-leather chairs in front of her desk, "it would be nice if you'd stop looking at me as if I were some new species of bug that had just crawled into your flower beds."

28

"That will be difficult, Mr. Jameson, since that is exactly how I perceive you."

"As a threat?" Rand asked.

Nicole glared at him. "No, as a new species of bug."

This wasn't going well at all. Rand gritted his teeth, smiling graciously, and took another stab at being civil. "May I call you Nicole?"

"You may not."

His smile disappeared. "Look, Nicole, this animosity between us is exactly why I'm here. I mean, we're essentially in the same business, right?" Rand asked, rather proud of himself for managing to sound so reasonable. "We are most certainly competitors, but that doesn't mean we can't deal with each other in a rational, even friendly—"

"Mr. Jameson," said Nicole, interrupting him. "My family has been in this business for a very long time. We are growers who have had to import to stay alive, while you are an importer who seems bent on cutting us out," she explained curtly. "How can you possibly expect us to be friends?"

"I'm not just an importer," he objected. "I buy plenty of American product, yours included."

Nicole pursed her lips in irritation. "I hate that term *product*. We deal in cut flowers, Jameson."

"That's one of your problems, Sabine," he returned just as irritably, settling back into the chair and crossing his long legs. "You're too passionately involved in what you do. Cut flowers are a product, just like any other, something to buy and sell and make a profit on. You growers are too sentimental."

"Who are you to lecture me?" Too upset to sit still, Nicole got up and went to the window overlooking the greenhouses. "Your company is a newborn compared to ours."

Rand stayed where he was, part of his mind registering her graceful walk, the sensuality of her full lips even when pursed in anger. She was almost too slender, yet with nice hips and the promise of firm, well-shaped breasts in outline beneath her pale pink blouse. He forced himself to ignore her earthy charm and concentrate. Establishing some kind of rapport with this woman was going to be harder than he first thought.

"Granted. But compared to me, your importing operation is in its infancy as well. What I'm saying, Nicole, is that rather than trying to tear each other apart, perhaps we could learn from each other."

Nicole turned from the window, a thin smile on her lips. "But I'm already learning from you, Jameson. One couldn't buy a better teacher in sharp business practices than you. I may well be an infant as an importer, but I'm growing day by day." *And I'll get you yet,* she thought, but she said to him, "You'd be better off tending your own fields rather than coming here, trying to learn more about mine."

Rand raised his eyebrows. For some insane reason her haughty determination made him even more anxious to get to know her.

"There is plenty of room for both of us. Why should we scratch and claw at each other? I'm not proposing a partnership, you know, just a better working relationship."

Nicole didn't know what to make of him. The Sabines had been aware of Rand Jameson, working on the periphery of the business, making a name for himself. When it had become necessary to butt heads with him, she had found out how tough, wily, and ruthless he could be.

Now he came to her with an apparently sincere desire to forge some kind of understanding, a competitive agreement, perhaps. It didn't fit with her mental image of him, but then she was adult enough to realize that image was to a certain extent based upon family prejudice. He wasn't a grower. He was different from them and therefore not to be trusted.

Nicole probably never would trust him. But actually she was the first Sabine to talk with him face-to-face. And it was a nice face. Her sister was right; Rand was definitely cute.

Frowning, she cut off that thought and returned to her desk, looking at him warily as she took a seat. It occurred to her that if his offer was genuine, she could make a giant stride toward a more secure future for the Sabine operation. At the very least she owed it to the family to put aside her animosity for a while and hear him out.

"All right, Mr. Jameson," she said, leaning

back in her chair and forcing herself to calm down. "Let's say I agree in principle. It would be good for both of us if we understood each other better. I'd like to know more about your operation, and I think you could use an education in a grower's concerns as well."

Rand grinned. She was something else. Even when she was being reasonable, she could manage to backhand him. "I agree," he said.

"Where would you like to start?"

"To begin with," he replied, standing up and offering her his hand, "my first name is Rand. It would please me if you would use it—and if I could reciprocate without getting another of those killer looks of yours, Nicole."

Nicole couldn't help smiling. Maybe they could work something out, after all.

"All right." She reached out and shook hands with him. His grip was strong. An unnerving tingle shot through her. "What did you have in mind, Rand?"

He shrugged. "How about a tour?"

With as much congeniality as was possible under the circumstances, and still feeling a vague sense of betraying family secrets, Nicole showed Rand around Sabine. Word had passed quickly through the operation, and as often as not, they found themselves with plenty of covert company.

"What do they think I'm going to do?" Rand asked tersely. "Assassinate you?"

Nicole chuckled. "Even the ones who aren't Sabines are like part of the family. You're some-

32

thing of an infamous personage to us, Rand. People get like that when someone threatens their livelihoods."

"It's not all that bad," he commented in an offended tone. "I'm just making a living like they are."

As she led him into yet another greenhouse some workers harvesting carnations paused to mutter among themselves and cast disdainful glances in Rand's direction.

"It *was* that bad, for a while. Not that those times were all your fault or even the competition's fault as a whole," Nicole informed him. "Heating these greenhouses in winter isn't cheap, and it's getting more expensive all the time. Inflation made it necessary to increase salaries to get and hold good workers. But those are factors that are hard to pin a name on."

"So was the sharp increase in imports, though. That was just an economic factor, a fluctuation in the money market more than anything. It's calmed down a lot."

"It has calmed down. And, unlike a lot of others, we were able to make changes and ride out the storm. Watch your step," she warned, grinning as he placed one of his polished loafers in a muddy puddle on the greenhouse floor. "But as an aggressive importer, you hit us hard. That was a factor with a face, so to speak, so yours became the likeness pinned to a lot of people's dart boards, including mine."

Rand looked at his mud-splattered shoe with

disdain. "I think I've seen enough of the farm," he said dryly.

"Okay. I'll show you our shipping department."

"I'd appreciate it. My drivers say it's quite efficient."

"It has to be," Nicole said, her voice full of sarcasm. "Yours is."

They left the greenhouse area and strolled across a stretch of graveled roadway to another large redbrick building. Rand tried to ignore the distinct impression she had that he was being both followed and watched.

"It's really hard for me to understand the growing side of the business," he said, looking back over his shoulder at the greenhouses. "I mean, why put up with the headache?"

"I don't expect you'll ever understand it, Rand," she replied, leading the way into the warehouse. It was much cooler there. "We're growers. We'll always be growers, even if it means cutting back on everything else and selling our flowers from corner stands, the way my grandfather's grandfather did in France."

"Tradition?" Rand asked.

She shook her head with something akin to pity. "It's more than tradition, it's a way of life. Don't feel bad. Even some of the family doesn't understand," Nicole told him. "All I can say is that if it's in your blood, you can't change. Somewhere, somehow, there will always be a Sabine growing flowers."

Rand watched as a couple of workers boxed cut flowers for shipment, layer upon layer separated by newspapers and wooden cleats to hold the stems down. It wasn't something the uninitiated were aware of, but flowers weren't nearly as fragile as they looked. Boxed like this, Sabine would truck them in refrigerated vehicles all over the state or even across the country, and they would arrive fresh and beautiful, ready for the florist's display case.

"I'd give my eyeteeth for a cooler this size," Rand said when she gave him a quick look at the refrigeration unit and their inventory on hand.

Nicole was mildly surprised. "Yours is much smaller?"

"Much," he answered, laughing. His breath made tiny puffs of vapor in the chill air. "Though the florists seem to think it's limitless."

She laughed with him. "Isn't that the truth? They're spoiled around this part of the country. They can live out of our coolers without taking any risks, knowing they don't have to buy until they're desperate because one of us wholesalers will always have something to send them."

"You see?" Rand stepped closer to her so she could hear him over the dull roar of the cooling pumps, looking into a beautiful, intelligent pair of gray-green eyes. "We're not all that different, you and I. At least not on this end."

Nicole cleared her throat, a nervous sound in the echoing cooler. She could feel the heat of his body, smell the pleasant masculine tang of his after-shave mingling with the muted fragrance of the cut flowers surrounding them.

"I . . . I guess not." He had nice eyes, a soft, warm shade of hazel. "Is there anything else you'd like to see?"

His gaze dropped to the curve of her throat, then lower, lingering on the soft swell of her breasts. Her nipples had grown hard in the cold air, small, tempting buds pushing against the material of her blouse. Was there something else he'd like to see?

"I'll say," Rand muttered hoarsely.

"Excuse me?"

He returned his gaze to her face, grinning at the momentary look of feminine vulnerability in her eyes. But the lapse in her armor was gone as quickly as it had come.

"I don't suppose you'd let me look at your client lists?"

Nicole blinked, then realized he was joking. She laughed and led the way out of the cooler. "Fat chance, Jameson," she replied sardonically, more than happy to return to open spaces and their wary banter.

She had seen something in his eyes she didn't like. Or did she? On an elemental level, somewhere deep inside her, she realized she was quite attracted to Rand. But it was an impossible situation. She'd rather take up with Attila the Hun than a man who had contributed so much to her family's near undoing.

Handsome or not, surprising congeniality and

humor aside, Rand Jameson was the competition, and she had better remember that fact. Maybe they weren't as different as it had first seemed, but they were still rivals, and they would be until the bitter end.

"I assume this door swings both ways, Rand. It's your turn to tell me about your operation."

He shrugged. "Sure, but it's pretty much like the last half of yours, really. I'll be glad to show you around if you'd like to stop by sometime."

"I'll do that."

"Good." He smiled at her. "Say, you wouldn't have a candy machine in that lunchroom I passed on the way in, would you?" he asked. "I skipped lunch today." He also wanted an excuse to continue chatting. He couldn't leave until he'd gotten what he came for.

Nicole returned his smile. "Me too. I'll join you. And you don't have to eat junk. We have a sandwich machine there too."

"Sounds great."

They took a shortcut through an adjoining greenhouse where Rand saw something that caught his eye. He stopped in front of Vin's private solarium.

"What's this?"

"Grandfather's orchids," Nicole replied uneasily. Through the translucent walls she could see Vin moving around inside the hothouse. He wouldn't understand Rand's presence there. "But—"

"Orchids!" Rand exclaimed. "I didn't know Sabine grew orchids."

"*We* don't. They're strictly my grandfather's concern, and he doesn't like to be disturbed. Let's go get that sandwich. . . ." Her voice trailed off in horror as he opened the door and stepped into the solarium before she could stop him. "Don't—"

"Whew! Humid in here."

Nicole shrugged in resignation and followed him in. She supposed Vin deserved a crack at him too. "Hello, Vin. We have a visitor."

Vin was bent over one of his precious beauties. He didn't even look up. "Shut the door," he demanded curtly. "And come look at this."

The pair did as requested. Nicole was used to the humidity of the place, but beads of perspiration were already forming on Rand's forehead. Rather enjoying his discomfort, she smiled and peered over her grandfather's shoulder.

"Look at what?" she asked.

"This!" Vin replied, pointing to a spot on the prize flower's foliage. "What does that look like to you?"

"Hmm," Nicole hummed thoughtfully. "Thrips damage?"

"That is what I think too." He carefully removed the plant from among the others and placed it in a separate glass enclosure. "Into the infirmary, my love. I am so worried. What if they have spread?"

"The others are very healthy, Vin. They'll fight

38

them off. Don't worry," she murmured sympathetically, patting him gently on the shoulder.

Rand looked at the older man, then at Nicole, a bewildered expression on his face. "Why not just spray the whole lot of them with insecticide?"

"Who is this man?" Vin roared, noticing Rand's presence for the first time. "An infusion of shag tobacco is the thing. Insecticide? Bah!" He stepped over to him, practically touching Rand's nose with his own. "Do I know you?" he asked with unconcealed hostility.

"Vin, this is Rand Jameson," Nicole said, staying well out of the way. "Rand, meet my grandfather, Vincent Sabine."

"You!" Vin exclaimed.

Taken aback by the old man's furious reaction, it was all Rand could do to extend his hand and say, "Pleased to meet you."

Vin didn't take his hand. He didn't even acknowledge the offer. "No doubt you are. Like the fox is happy to meet the chicken. What is your business here?" he asked, taking a step back and looking at the younger man with great suspicion. "Espionage?"

"Not at all." This was the patriarch, the Sabine from whom Nicole had obviously gotten her mental toughness. If Rand could get on some kind of even ground with him, it would improve his chances with her. "I simply thought it was time for me to meet my stiffest competitor face-to-face. Nicole and I agreed that if we knew each other better, we might be able to tone down this rivalry between us."

"Tone down?" Vin looked at Nicole. *"Qu'est-ce que c'est,* tone down?"

"Smooth out the rough edges, Vin," she explained. "Rand came here to make peace with us. Supposedly," she added, looking at Rand with a wry smile.

Rand nodded. "That's right. Make peace."

"Why?"

"We don't have to dig at each other, do we?" Rand asked.

Vin's bushy gray eyebrows shot up. "But of course we do! We are enemies, are we not?"

"We don't have to be."

"You agree with this, Nicole?" he asked her.

She shrugged, her arms folded over her breasts. "Perhaps. I'm waiting, Vin. Waiting and watching."

"Good," he said, apparently satisfied. "We all trust your judgment, Nicole." Vin pointed at Rand. "You, we will never trust. Smooth edges or not, we will always be enemies. The Sabines are like elephants. We may forgive but we never forget." Turning back to his orchids, he dismissed them both with a crisp, "I have work to do," and apparently forgot they were even there.

It wasn't until Nicole and Rand were in the lunchroom, sharing a chicken salad sandwich and drinking coffee, that Rand regained his balance and ventured a comment on his meeting with Vin.

"Rather a character, isn't he?"

Nicole chuckled. "Rather." Vin was right, though. They were enemies and probably always would be, despite any changes they might make. Why was a part of her wishing it wasn't so? "He's brusque with everybody, though, so don't take it to heart. And you caught him at a bad time. His orchids are everything to him now."

"I can see why. They're beautiful," Rand said.

Nicole gazed at him curiously. "I thought you said flowers were just a product. What happened to your opinion of grower's sentimentality?"

"Maybe the tour helped," Rand replied. "Not that I understand completely. As you said, I probably never will. But I think I've gotten a feel for your emotional attachment to your product . . . I mean, your flowers," he amended quickly.

She laughed yet still felt as if he had something he wanted to say. "But . . ."

"But it's time for that door you spoke of to swing the other way, I think," he said. "I'd like to offer a small suggestion."

"Oh?"

"I realize you must consider the foreign growers as kinfolk of a kind. I don't think that's such a great idea. Get as attached to your own flowers as you want, but treat the imports as nothing more than a product."

"Seems like sound advice."

Nicole decided not to tell him that his advice had already been implemented in a way. Hiring professional salespeople was one of the changes

41

she had instigated that had made Sabine better able to compete with Rand and his ilk.

It felt good, though, hearing from him that her decision had been a sound one. The family hadn't thought so, until the profits increased. She realized that talking to a businessman like Rand was a pleasant change from arguing with Vin or her father. Rand understood the necessity of a multifaceted approach to wholesaling.

"You agree, then?" he asked, surprised.

Nicole nodded. "I just about have to, don't I? Most of their flowers are government-subsidized, and they cooperate with each other," she replied. "That gives them enough of an edge over us free-enterprising Americans."

"That's right. We have to stick together too," he said nonchalantly, seeing an opening and going for it right away. "America can grow flowers as good or better than anything coming out of Europe. I'm heavy into imports, as you well know—"

"Do I ever," she interjected dryly.

"But I like to cut them out when I can," Rand continued, unperturbed. "It's nice to see growers such as yourself getting into the fight, switching to exotic crops, making it attractive to buy from you."

"It isn't easy, though, believe me," Nicole muttered. Then she looked at him, eyes wide with surprise. "I'm having a hard time believing what I'm hearing. If what you're telling me is true, why don't you buy more from me?"

Rand shrugged. "Business. I'm not going to tell you my profit margin. When you give me a price that works for me, I buy." He looked at her slyly. "How about you? Why is it I find that after I buy from you I go to one of my clients and find you've already sold them at a price I can't beat?" he asked, grinning broadly.

"Business," she replied airily. "I'm not going to tell you my profit margin, either."

They laughed together. An employee came into the room to get a soda from the machine and looked at them, obviously astonished. Was that the boss and Rand Jameson, actually sharing a sandwich and appearing to enjoy each other's company? He went out shaking his head and muttering to himself.

"I think we're spoiling our images," Rand commented.

"Could be. Could be they need spoiling."

The man was not an ogre. Nicole still didn't trust him an inch but was feeling better about the future than she had in some time. It just might be that Rand really was trying to make peace. Her world had gotten brighter.

"So," he said casually, "when can you make it over so I can show you how the other half lives?"

"Maybe tomorrow. I never know if I'm going to have any free time until after the morning rush dies down."

"Same here." He finished his coffee and stood up as if to go. Then, as if it were an afterthought, he said, "Say, I noticed you have quite a few

43

sweetheart roses right now. I've got some space in my cooler I wouldn't mind filling if I can get a good deal."

Nicole frowned. There was something that bothered her about Rand Jameson coming here out of the blue, offering the hand of friendship then subtly asking about this month's hottest property. Her frown disappeared, to be replaced slowly by a knowing smile.

"Need them pretty badly, don't you?" she asked.

It was quite a battle to continue looking innocent, but Rand managed. "Not at all," he said in his best matter-of-fact tone. "I just saw that you had them on hand and thought maybe we could do some business. If you don't want to sell . . ." He trailed off and started to turn away.

"I didn't say that." She kept her face placid even though she wanted to chuckle. He was one cool customer, but something had him hot and bothered. "I'm selling if you're buying."

"How much?" Rand asked, as if he couldn't care less. She quoted him a figure and he grabbed his throat dramatically. "I thought we were starting to get along."

"Business, remember?" she returned sweetly. "What kind of figure did you have in mind?" When he told her, she started laughing. "Are you crazy? I have retailers begging for my little roses. Why should I sell to you for half of what I can get from them?"

"A goodwill gesture?" Rand offered hopefully.

Nicole shook her head, still chuckling. "That wouldn't be a goodwill gesture. That would be a very big favor, and I don't owe you a thing, Jameson."

"All right." Rand returned to the table and sat back down, glaring at her, his face grim. "Maybe we can work something out."

"Maybe," Nicole said doubtfully.

She wasn't just tough, she was smart. He was glad he had come; he'd learned a few things, but she had caught him and that was that. It was quite obvious that she was enjoying having him in this position, and he'd simply have to live with her glee. The ray of hope was that she seemed willing to negotiate, a first for their dealings together.

"I need them, okay?" he told her acidly. "A shipment fell through, and I'm stuck between a rock and a hard place."

"Poor baby."

"Lord, you're really having a good time, aren't you?"

"You bet." She smiled. "Now, since there's no way for me to know if you're telling the truth should I ask you the minimum price you can accept," she said thoughtfully, "I propose a trade."

Rand looked at her warily, his eyes narrowing. "What kind of trade?"

"Well . . ." She thought quickly. "I heard from a little birdie that you have a shipment of auratum lilies arriving tomorrow."

"What little birdie?" Rand demanded.

45

"You know those New York brokers. They all seem to know each other, and everybody else too," Nicole replied. "It doesn't matter. What matters is that I have been waiting for quite some time to break into the market for that particular product," she said, pointedly not calling them flowers. "Somebody has been keeping me closed out."

"Poor baby," he returned, smiling without humor.

"I want in on that shipment."

"No. If I let you in, you'll end up selling to some of my clients and they might look to you next time instead of me."

"You want the roses, right?" she asked. "You even said you were between a rock and a hard place, as a matter of fact."

Rand sighed. She had him and she knew it. "All right, all right. How many of them do you want?" She told him. "Are you kidding? That's a third of the shipment!" he cried.

"I know."

"You—"

"Careful, Rand, or I'll stick you with a surcharge on the sweethearts to boot," Nicole warned. "Of course, you could always get them out of Chicago or California, maybe Pittsburgh." She laughed gleefully at the scowl on his face. "Oh, I forgot. You probably couldn't pay freight and break even, could you?"

"You know damn well I can't, you unfeeling chunk of granite."

"Me?" She batted her eyelashes. "I'm a sentimental grower, remember? Actually I think I've changed my mind. I don't think I want to sell my lovely roses to you," Nicole said with a vindictive grin. "I'll just wait until you fall flat on your face and sell them to your client myself."

"You don't know who it is," he countered.

She shrugged. "No, but I'm sure they know me. Maybe they won't get as good a price from me, but I bet they'll pay. And they'll remember who let them down too."

"You learn fast, Sabine," Rand grumbled.

"I've had a good teacher, Jameson," Nicole returned. "Maybe I'm not such an infant, after all."

Rand had a very good description of what she was, but he kept it to himself. "Enough. You want in on the shipment, you're in. Satisfied?"

"Straight trade," she said, her smile gone. "After they're cleared through customs in New York and *my* broker cuts the air bill, we'll take delivery together, at your place, so I can look them over myself."

"Why?"

"If you think I'm going to sit here twiddling my thumbs while you pretend to lose the shipment or pick through it and send me the dross—"

Rand stood up and glared at her. "I don't work that way, Nicole. I make a deal, I stick to it. How about you? Am I going to get the lowest-grade flowers you can cut?"

"You'll get top-grade," she assured him, standing up so she could look him in the eye. "I stick to my deals too."

They glowered at each other for a moment. Then Rand extended his hand. Nicole hesitantly extended her own, and they shook on the deal.

"Pleasure doing business with you, Nicole," he said sarcastically.

"The pleasure is all mine," she returned with a bitter smile of triumph.

"This time." He inclined his head slightly, a bow of acknowledgment for her victory, then released her hand and pointed his finger at her like the barrel of a pistol. "Next time, though . . ."

Nicole chuckled. "Nothing has changed, Rand. We've been gunning for each other for a long time." A smile played across her full lips. "Come to think of it, I suppose we kind of like it that way, don't we?"

"I suppose we do, at that, Nicole," he replied, smiling in spite of himself. He turned to leave. "I'll be in touch."

"Of course you will. I've got your product."

She watched as he went out the door shaking his head. A giddy laugh bubbled from her throat. She felt good all over, a sensation she cherished as she practically danced up the stairs to the office. At long last Sabine had gotten one step ahead of Rand Jameson, and Nicole vowed to keep it that way from now on.

CHAPTER THREE

Jameson Wholesale Floral wasn't quite what Nicole was used to. For one thing, there wasn't a greenhouse in sight, nor did Rand's business spread across acres of land, as did Sabine. His was a simple operation, little more than a warehouse, really, set among others just like it in an industrial district near the airport. *Functional* was the word that came to mind.

At the moment, however, as she parked her car at the loading dock and gathered her wits about her, Nicole had only one thing on her mind. Mayhem. How could she have been so stupid as to trust Rand to live up to a bargain?

She was dressed for battle today, in taupe slacks and a soft yellow long-sleeved blouse with an overlay handkerchief neckline. Businesslike yet feminine.

Her high heels clicked on the concrete floor as she strode into the warehouse. Empty boxes and folded newspapers lay scattered around, evidence that her delivery had long since arrived, been unpacked, and then loaded into Rand's trucks for dispersal to his clients. It made Nicole even madder; the roses she'd sent him were already gone. Like a fool, she had filled his order in good faith, while behind her back he had been planning treachery all along.

Sitting at a battered desk near the door to his cooler, checking off items on an order list, Rand didn't hear Nicole's approach over the throb of the refrigeration unit until she was right on top of him. He looked up, surprised, his eyes opening even wider when he saw her furious expression.

"Hi, Nicole," he said in a bewildered tone. Maybe she'd had trouble with the midday traffic. This neighborhood was a jungle at noon. "You look like you've had a bad morning. Coffee?" he asked, pointing to a machine set up on the corner of the desk.

"Weasel!" she said, her teeth clenched. "How dare you make polite conversation?"

Rand looked her over. It was a cliché, but she was beautiful when she was angry. Spots of color had appeared on her high cheekbones, emphasizing her otherwise pale complexion. Her eyes flashed. Even the fact that her anger was directed at him couldn't spoil his appreciation of how vibrant she looked as she tossed her head, blond hair bouncing around her face.

"You seem in a pretty good state of pique," he commented, trying not to smile too broadly. "Is something wrong?"

Nicole became aware that she was so mad, she was huffing and puffing, and that Rand was enjoying the way her breasts strained against her blouse as she did so. To think she had actually started to like the man!

"You . . . how can you just sit there and . . ." Nicole trailed off and glared at him. "Stop ogling me like that!"

"I can't help it. Seeing you all worked up like this, well, it makes me realize what a passionate nature you have, Nicole." He grinned. "Of course, outrage wouldn't have been my first choice of emotions, but—"

"I don't believe this!" she interrupted. "What kind of man cheats a woman one minute then makes a pass at her the next?"

Rand stood up abruptly, even more confused. "Cheat you? What are you talking about?"

"You really are a reptile, Rand," she said, taking a step backward. "Are you going to stand there and tell me you're not pulling some quick switch with the shipment?"

"Yes."

"What?"

"I'm telling you I don't have the faintest idea what you're driving at, Nicole," he replied, getting a bit angry himself now. He looked at his watch. "The shipment should have arrived in New York this morning. Are you saying it didn't? What's going on?"

Nicole stared at him, a sinking feeling in the pit of her stomach. "You don't know? You really don't know?"

"How could I?" Rand said sarcastically. "You

insisted on using your broker, remember? Why should he call me?"

She turned away, squeezing her eyes shut. It wasn't bad enough she had jumped to conclusions. She had to come here and embarrass herself in front of him. "I thought—"

"I'm beginning to get a pretty good idea what you thought," Rand shot back. He grabbed her arm and turned her back to face him. "We have a deal, Nicole. I agreed to share the shipment with you and I will. Those auratum lilies should be somewhere between New York and here at this very moment. If they're not, don't blame me. I told you we should have used my broker."

"You mean, you didn't tell him to take over?" she asked.

"Of course I didn't!" Rand stared hard at her. "Where are the flowers, Nicole?"

"Still at JFK," she said, then added, "I think."

"What!" Rand roared indignantly.

"Don't you yell at me, Rand Jameson. When my broker went to oversee the transfer and customs inspection, he was told your guy had already taken charge."

"He did not!"

"Somebody did!"

"What the . . ." Rand let go of her arm and started toward a flight of stairs at the back of the warehouse. Nicole followed. "What kind of imbecile have you got up there, anyway? Have they been off-loaded?"

"Yes, but—"

"Then what's the hang-up?" he asked, opening a door at the top of the stairs and ushering her into a large room filled with desks and other office paraphernalia. "Customs?"

Nicole couldn't meet his eyes. "I don't know."

"What do you mean, you don't know?"

"You see, when my broker called and told me what had happened, I naturally thought you were pulling a fast one and I—"

"Naturally." Rand sat down behind one of the desks and blew out an exasperated breath. "Apology accepted."

"I wasn't apologizing!"

"Would you quit blithering and tell me the whole story?"

So she had been wrong. He didn't know what was going on. Nicole still wanted to strangle him. "I guess the, um, shipment is sort of lost."

"It's what?" Suddenly the room seemed very quiet.

"If your broker didn't get them, and mine didn't . . ."

Rand rubbed his face with his hands and sighed. "Lord. My life was relatively simple a few days ago. How could you have complicated it so quickly?"

"Oh, really. It's all my fault now, is it?" Nicole asked sarcastically. "May I remind you who saved you from financial trauma with those roses?"

"Just shut up and call your broker, will you?" Rand muttered.

In spite of their predicament, Nicole managed to smile vindictively at the chagrined look on his face, then picked up the phone and dialed. Rand watched, tense.

"Hello, Alfredo. Any news?" Her eyebrows arched. "Really? What happened?" As she listened to the import broker's explanation relief spread slowly across Nicole's face. Rand glowered at her impatiently. "I see. Thanks."

When she had hung up the phone, she leaned back in the chair in front of Rand's desk and looked up at the ceiling. Why couldn't Alfredo have found the shipment *before* she had come charging over here? The news was good, but it was also bad in a way. Now she really did have an apology to make to Rand. Nicole imagined it would stick in her throat.

"Well?" he demanded.

"I feel not unlike a fool," she replied.

Rand chuckled. "I guess that means they straightened everything out?"

"Evidently it was a busy morning. The shipment got shuttled to the wrong holding area, and the confusion was compounded by the fact that you were listed as the importer, while my broker was supposed to handle things." She managed to look at him. "Sorry."

"It wasn't your fault," he said, suddenly feeling very magnanimous. Yesterday she had had the upper hand. Today the shoe was on the other foot. "These things happen."

"I know. I mean, I'm sorry for coming over here foaming at the mouth."

"Oh, that's all right." Rand winked at her rakishly. "Like I said, it gave me a look at your passionate nature."

"Passionately crazy."

He shrugged. "Passion's passion. I'll take what I can get, for now."

"What's that supposed to—"

"So," Rand interrupted, "the shipment's on its way?"

She nodded and got to her feet. "They're getting ready to load right now. I'll call Alfredo in a couple of hours, make sure there weren't any more hitches."

"Good." He stood up. "While we're waiting, how about a tour and then some lunch?" he asked quickly, coming around the desk and taking her by the arm. "I know this terrific restaurant not far from here, built inside an old airplane hangar."

"Well . . ."

"How can you refuse? When we get back, you can put the call to Alfredo on my phone bill."

Thankful for the opportunity to put her embarrassment behind her, Nicole agreed, following Rand as he showed her the warehouse. She easily could see why he was so able to undercut her. His operation was bare bones, all muscle and efficiency, just like the man himself. As he had said the day before, they didn't operate all that differently; it was just that he didn't have as many mouths to feed or property taxes and heating bills to pay.

Judging by her tirade earlier, she was obviously prepared to distrust him at the drop of a hat, but she couldn't deny her attraction to him. In fact, as they talked over lunch, she spent a few secret moments just looking at him, listening to his confident voice, wondering what other interesting things they might find along the way to a better business relationship.

"Didn't you have a garden shop and nursery over at your place for a while?" Rand asked. "I think there's an apartment complex or something on the land now."

"That was my uncle. Grandfather split his property between his sons when he retired," Nicole explained. "Vin practically disowned him when he sold out to the developers. There's still some animosity between them, but they get along okay. Two of his kids even work for us part-time, while they go to college."

"A Sabine may forgive, but they never forget," Rand said, recalling her grandfather's warning when they had met yesterday. "Is Vin anywhere near as tough as he looks and sounds?"

She nodded. "Every bit," she replied, then looked at him slyly. "As you may have noticed, quick tempers seem to run in the family. You're lucky my mother and father are on vacation or you probably would have seen theirs too."

"Forget it. Considering our history, it's amazing we're talking, let alone having lunch together.

I'm glad we are, though. I think coming over to see you yesterday was one of my better decisions."

"Even if you ended up having to share a shipment?"

Rand laughed. "All right. So I had ulterior motives. You're sharper than I thought you were, and I'm paying for underestimating you, but I'm still glad we finally met." He looked at her curiously, a definite gleam in his eyes. "Aren't you?"

"I'm still watching and waiting," she replied.

"This could be the start of something good, Nicole."

Did he mean business or something else? From the way he was looking at her, his eyes full of undeniable masculine interest, she was getting the distinct impression he wasn't talking about an improved working relationship.

"Could be," she said with a shrug that belied her confused emotions. "If this deal works out, who knows?"

"That's right. Who knows?"

Then he reached across the table and put his hand atop hers. No doubt about it. Rand was letting her know he would like to become much more than her adversary. Nicole didn't know how she felt about the message he was trying to convey. She did know she was still getting danger signals. A lot more trust would have to develop between them before she lowered her guard.

That didn't mean, however, that she was immune to his touch. Far from it, in fact. She moved her hand away from his and cleared her throat nervously. "I must admit to some surprise concerning the size of your business," she told him. "For as much trouble as you've caused me, I somehow expected a larger operation."

A small smile tugged at the corners of Rand's mouth, but he accepted the change of subject. "Ten employees, most of whom pull double duty, sales as well as warehouse and delivery," he said. "That and a batch of phone lines is all it takes."

"And a little skill."

He shrugged. "We've done well. It is about time for another change of address. Next year at this time maybe we'll be as big as you expected."

"What a terrifying thought," Nicole commented dryly.

"I don't see why. There's room for both of us."

"Is there?"

Rand looked at her, perturbed. "What are you getting at, Nicole?"

"Just something a salesman of mine and I were, um, discussing the other day." She looked at him pointedly. "Are you retailing, Rand?"

"Are you?" he countered.

Nicole straightened in her chair as if she'd received an electric jolt. "How dare you!"

"I could have reacted with the same righteous indignation," Rand said placidly. "But I'm honest enough to admit I've been tempted. With the markup, who wouldn't be? And some retailers are quick enough to bypass flower brokers like me and go directly to growers like you, aren't they?"

"Well, yes, but I'm a broker too, and—"

"You've put your finger on it, Nicole. The boundaries aren't as clear as they used to be. Once upon a time there was a chain: grower to wholesaler to retailer to consumer. Things have changed, not just in our business but in every business."

Her cloudy expression cleared, and she sighed. "I know. Importers, exporters, direct-sales operations. It is hard to know where one stands these days," she agreed. "We've even got people like Alfredo now, who don't know flowers or chocolates or the thousand other things they handle but are experts in getting the stuff through customs and smoothly onto trucks and planes." Nicole looked at him sharply and added, "But I don't retail."

"Neither do I."

They glared at each other for a moment, then chuckled and clinked their glasses of iced tea together in a mutual toast. Nicole felt an odd kind of camaraderie forming between them. Would wonders never cease?

"To competition," she said, "and to us dinosaurs trying to survive in a world gone amok."

"Here, here," Rand agreed with a humorously somber expression. "Shall we sing patriotic songs now?"

"People would stare."

"Just the communist spies." He leaned closer

to her and said in a conspiratorial tone, "They're everywhere, you know."

"How can you tell?" she whispered back.

"They wear buttons."

"Buttons? Like what?"

"Buy direct!" he informed her. "Down with the middleman!"

"The fiends!"

They left the restaurant laughing, arm in arm, a sight that would have given her family a group seizure had they been there to see it. Nicole wasn't quite sure yet, but she had the suspicion she and Rand could become friends.

What more might come from this business liaison remained to be seen. For now she was content to savor her triumph; the shipment would soon be here and she would receive the cut she had earned by besting Rand in a fair fight. She felt light and alive. If the source of her happiness had more to do with Rand and his intriguing interest in her than in completing this deal, she would know soon enough.

"None the worse for wear, I'm happy to say," Rand said as he looked over the shipment. "Beautiful, aren't they?"

"Fabulous," Nicole agreed, unwrapping a bundle of the rare auratum lilies and admiring the huge white blooms. A yellow stripe ran down each creamy petal, and she traced the paths gently. "Hello, you little money-makers. Did you have a nice flight?"

"Lord, I've created a monster," he said, laughing heartily. "You're developing a pretty mercenary attitude for a sentimental grower, Nicole."

She ignored him and carefully selected her share of the shipment, directing the two employees she had brought with her to load the carton into a Sabine van. Because of the delay, it was late, and Rand's crew had gone home right after they had shuttled the cut flowers here from the airport. Nicole was anxious to get her drivers off the clock as well.

"Thanks for filling in, Tony," she told the young salesman. "Just get these into our cooler and you can call it a day."

"Sure thing, boss. See you tomorrow."

Nicole watched as he and his helper climbed into the van, then pulled away from the dock into the cloudy twilight. Hopefully the rain would hold off until they got home. She turned to Rand, her hand extended.

"Pleasure doing business with you, Jameson," she said with a wry smile.

He shook her hand but didn't let go of it right away. "Same here, Sabine. And this time I mean it."

"Your wounded pride has mended?" she asked. "That was fast. When I left you after lunch, you seemed to be pouting."

"I was pouting," he informed her. "But not over my pride." He released her hand to caress her arm, smiling at her shivering response to his

61

gentle touch. "I like being with you, Nicole. Have dinner with me?"

"I—I can't," she replied.

This was crazy! She barely knew him, and aside from the surprises of the last two days, the things she did know about him were hardly assuring. He hadn't gotten where he was in this business by being a nice guy.

"I have a ton of paperwork to do," Nicole informed him. It was a convenient excuse, and it happened to be true. "I'll probably just grab a sandwich from the machine and slave at my desk until midnight."

"You work too hard," he said softly.

Nicole's eyes widened in alarm as he took a casual step closer to her. Mesmerized, she requested her feet to move but they flatly refused, and she felt the heat of his body next to hers. There was definitely something about him that played havoc with her body chemistry.

"Don't, Rand," she told him, annoyed with her voice for failing her. She cleared her throat. "You can't wipe out years of mistrust in two days."

"I suppose not," he murmured, his head moving closer to hers, aiming for those full, ripe lips, which seemed to taunt him every time she spoke. "I have work to do, too, I guess."

He was agreeing with her, but he was about to kiss her, The man was tricky, all right. Nicole's lips parted of their own volition, her neck arching back as she felt his warm breath upon her cheek. Her feet still refused to move.

"I really do have work to do," she whispered.

"Me too."

"I should be going."

Rand's lips were almost touching hers now. He said softly, "I think you'd probably better."

A loud clap of thunder announced the arrival of the storm that had been threatening all day. At last Nicole's feet obeyed her, and she took a step back from Rand, her eyes still locked to his. The air around her felt thick, electrified, and laden with moisture. Outside, the dark clouds opened up, and rain poured from the skies, a gust of wind pushing its way through the open warehouse door to caress her heated skin. She shivered but not because she was cold.

"That was close." Rand's voice was deep and throaty.

"Yes. The lightning was very close," she said, refusing to acknowledge what had almost happened. "This could be quite a storm."

He grinned. "Count on it."

"Well, I'd better get back and make sure everything's battened down." Now that her feet were moving, she hurried toward the door, not daring to look at him again. "I kind of like doing paperwork in the rain, though," she told him, realizing she was making small talk so he wouldn't have time to speak before she got outside. "If it's a nice night, I never want to work late. I should get a lot done this evening."

63

Rand was chuckling. "There are other nice things to do on rainy nights, Nicole."

Choosing to ignore his evident and tempting invitation, she waved without turning around and dashed into the downpour, dodging puddles as she made her way to her car. "Thanks, Rand. See you later," Nicole yelled.

"You can count on that too," he said to himself as he watched her drive off.

CHAPTER FOUR

Nicole sat in her office, the papers piled on her desk forgotten for the moment as she watched rain pelt against the window. Summer storms in this part of the country could be wicked, and this one seemed to be working itself up to a frenzy. As long as it only rained, though, she wasn't too worried. It was hail she dreaded, as anybody with as many greenhouses as Sabine naturally would. At least it wasn't like the old days Vin talked about. The new plastics held up much better than glass.

"Just keep it smaller than golf ball size, please," she muttered under her breath.

It was only with a great deal of discipline that she had managed to get any work done. Her thoughts kept drifting to Rand, their pleasant lunch that afternoon, and his amiable division of the shipment earlier in the evening. Of course, he'd almost kissed her, and she'd almost let him, but she tried to put that part out of her mind.

A noise startled her from her inwardly directed thoughts. She couldn't make out what it was at first, what with the roar of the rain and thunder outside. At last she realized it was someone pounding on the door downstairs and yelling her name. She grabbed her key ring and hurried to see who it was. Vin had probably walked over from his small house at the corner of the property to check on things, worried about the storm and his orchids. He always forgot his keys.

At the foot of the steps she could see a dark shape through the glass front doors, a man in a raincoat, too tall to be her grandfather, and sounding as mad as he was wet.

"Open up, Sabine!" He banged on the glass, rattling the doors. "Let me in, you . . ." Thunder obliterated his words, but he didn't look at all happy.

"Rand?" She fumbled her key into the lock and swung the doors open. "What are you doing here? You look like a drowned rat."

"The only rat around here is you," he announced angrily as he flung himself out of the rain. Water dripped off his slicker, pooling at his feet. "Why did you do it, Nicole? Everything was going so well."

She stared at him as if he were insane. He looked insane, his face a mask of anger as he peeled off his raincoat and threw it on the floor. Beneath it, his slacks and shirt were damp. Rainwater dribbled down wind-reddened cheeks from his sodden hair, adding to his crazed appearance.

Nicole instinctively drew away from him and

backed into the reception area. "What are you talking about?" she asked.

"You know very well what . . ." He trailed off, seeing the frightened expression on her face. "Damn. Now I'm doing it," Rand grumbled irritably. "Flying off the handle like you did earlier. I didn't know it was you. Maybe it was some of your disgruntled workers."

Recovering from her shock, Nicole put her hands on her hips and glared at him. "What was it I or my workers were supposed to have done?" she demanded.

"Wrecked my place!" he returned vehemently. "It's a mess. Flowers everywhere, torn up, trampled, and ruined. My dock looks like a flower bed would if somebody drove a threshing machine through it. My office isn't much better. Papers all over, filing cabinets dumped out." He stood there looking miserable for a moment, then turned his attention back to Nicole. "You're responsible!" he accused with renewed vigor.

"I would never do something like that! How dare you!" she responded indignantly.

"Your employees, then," he countered. "You said they hate me."

"There's no love lost there," she agreed. "But it's crazy, Rand. They wouldn't tear up your place. They're flower workers, not vandals. Besides, I'd fire them for that kind of destructive behavior and they know it."

Rand wiped his face off with his hands and leaned heavily against the wall. He looked tired.

Feeling a pang of sympathy, Nicole warily advanced a step toward him.

"I don't know," he muttered. "Whoever it was, they worked fast. I left about ten but came back at eleven to make sure the warehouse roof wasn't leaking. When I saw the mess, I went crazy." He looked at her. "I'm sorry for scaring you. The adrenaline is wearing off now."

"Come on. I've got hot coffee in my office and some paper towels. You'll catch your death."

When he had dried off and had a cup of steaming coffee in his hand, Rand looked as though he might survive, after all. His eyes, though, still burned with anger.

"I don't get it," he said tersely. "What were they after? I don't keep money there. They didn't take any of the office machines."

Nicole sipped thoughtfully at her coffee. "And they didn't steal any flowers? Those are worth money."

"Tell me about it. My stock is ruined," Rand said bitterly. "No, they didn't take any, as far as I could tell. Just ripped them stem from petal and scattered them all over the floor."

"Sounds like vandalism."

"Maybe."

"Have you called the police?" He shook his head. "Why, Rand, how sweet," she said sarcastically. "The first person you thought of was me."

He shrugged his shoulders in an apologetic gesture. "So sue me. You were right. We can't wipe out years of mistrust in a couple of days."

"Don't you think you'd better call them?" Nicole asked, sliding the phone across the desk to him.

"On a night like this they probably won't have the time to make it out, anyway."

Nicole looked at him, frowning slightly. He was right, of course, but why did it seem as if there were more to it than that? Maybe he didn't like policemen.

Her frown deepened. Or maybe he didn't really believe she and her staff were innocent and wanted to keep the cops out of what he viewed as a private vendetta. Perhaps he was already planning retribution.

"Shall I call them for you?" she asked, her expression stone-cold and suspicious.

Now Rand frowned. "I'm too tired. I'll do it tomorrow."

"Rand . . ." But the phone rang before she could voice her suspicions.

"What's wrong, Nicole?" he asked, staring at her warily. "Expecting a call you don't want me to hear?" His hand hovered over the receiver. "Do you want me to answer it?"

She grabbed the phone and pulled it back to her side of the desk. "Sure. Rand Jameson answering my phone at this time of night. If it's one of my family, they'd have the cops here in minutes, rain or no." *And maybe that's not such a bad idea,* she thought.

Nicole picked up the receiver and put it to her ear, then immediately yanked it away again.

"Slow down, Vin! And speak English. I can't understand you when you talk this fast. What? What flowers?" She looked up sharply at Rand. "I'll be right there, Vin."

"What's wrong?"

"No wonder you didn't want to call the police."

"I haven't the faintest idea—"

"Bull!" Nicole got up and went to the closet, pulling out a lime-green hooded rain slicker. "The first thing you thought of when you saw what somebody had done to your place was that we were responsible," she ground out through clenched teeth as she struggled into her raincoat. "The second thing you thought of was revenge. I hope you enjoyed yourself, Rand, because I'm going to sue your ears off."

She hurried from the room. Rand jumped up, grabbed his own coat, and ran after her, catching up with her at the foot of the stairs. He tried to take hold of her arm, but she pulled away.

"Don't touch me!"

"Nicole—"

"What happened, Rand?" she asked acidly. "Did you feel guilty after your little visit to my cooler? Is that why you decided to talk to me?"

Shrugging into his coat, Rand followed her out the front door, yelling to make himself heard over the pounding rain. "What visit to your cooler? I came right to your front door!" he objected.

Nicole wasn't listening. "No, a person like you doesn't feel guilt," she yelled into the darkness as she strode toward the shipping department. "You wanted to make it seem as if you had just arrived, so I wouldn't suspect you. Well, it won't work."

"Wait a minute, dammit!" Rand grabbed her again, and this time he held on, whirling her around to face him. "Are you saying somebody wrecked your inventory too?" he demanded, heedless of the rain pouring down around them.

Nicole glared at him, just able to make out his face in the gloom. "Stop it, Rand. I don't believe a thing you say. Not anymore."

She pushed away from him, slipping in the mud, almost falling to her knees. But she managed to regain her footing and continue on toward the pool of yellow light that marked the entrance to the brick building in front of them. Rand was right on her heels. He started to say more as they walked inside, but the sight before them silenced him immediately.

"Good Lord!" Nicole gasped.

"Just like my place," Rand muttered.

Flowers were strewn all over the concrete floor, ripped apart so thoroughly that it was hard to tell what kind they were. Shipping cartons had been shredded as well, bits and pieces of cardboard scattered everywhere. Order forms, bills of lading, and a dozen other sorts of documents spilled out of a nearby cubicle that served as an office, once the contents of a row of filing cabinets that had been dumped systematically. It was like something out of a hurricane disaster movie.

Amid the chaos Vin wandered, waving his

hands and muttering to himself. "Look at this! Who would do such a thing?" He shook his gray head sadly. "No souls. They must have no souls."

"He doesn't, Vin," Nicole said, staring at Rand.

Vin looked up, his eyes full of fury. "Jameson."

Rand scarcely noticed them. He was walking around the dock, occasionally prodding a pile of ruined flowers with the muddy toe of his shoe. The look on his face made Nicole frown. Was it possible for any man to pretend innocence this well?

"Auratum," he said to no one in particular. "Most of them are auratum lilies."

Nicole's eyes widened as she realized he was right. She had forgotten. Rand Jameson wasn't just any man. "Of course!" she gasped. "How could I be so stupid? I only have your word that somebody vandalized your place. You're trying to make it look like a conspiracy or something, aren't you? To throw suspicion off yourself for destroying my part of the shipment!"

"Come on," he shot back sarcastically. "Just to keep you from selling a few cut flowers? I'm not that petty, nor is my company on anything like shaky ground."

"You couldn't stand the thought of me winning, then," she returned. It sounded crazy even as she said it, but she was convinced he was capable of almost anything.

"Do you want to see my warehouse? I'll gladly show it to you. It looks just like this," Rand informed her, waving a hand at the destruction around them. "If you think I'd do that to myself as part of some scheme to get back at you, you really are stupid, Nicole."

Nicole frowned. He seemed to be telling the truth. But what did that leave? Conspiracy? It did look as if someone was trying to set them at each other's throats. But who would do such a thing, and why?

Vin's loud voice interrupted her thoughts. "Why are we listening to this man, Nicole? We should call the police."

"Good idea, Vin," she said, carefully observing Rand's reaction. To her great surprise he was nodding his head.

"Yes, it is a good idea," he agreed. "There's something going on here. Let's stop pointing fingers at each other and find out what."

Rand turned on his heel and went into the small office behind him, sorting through the rubble until he found the phone. While he talked to the police Nicole and her grandfather looked at each other in confusion.

"One would not expect a vandal to phone the police."

She shook her head. "No."

"He is a tricky one, Nicole."

"Very."

"Do you trust him?"

"Not an inch, Vin."

The old man nodded thoughtfully, then looked around him with disdain. "This is making me ill,

Nicole." He thought of the bottle of wine he had hidden in his hothouse and headed for the door. "I am going to look in on my orchids."

She smiled, knowing full well what he was up to. "Save me a glass. And don't stay up too late."

Rand returned from using the phone. "I was right. Nobody can make it out here tonight. A storm like this keeps them pretty busy, with wrecks and such."

"Convenient," Nicole muttered, looking out the door at the rain. It seemed to be slackening.

"I suppose you're going to accuse me of seeding the clouds now, right?" he asked in a sarcastic tone. "All part of my plan, so the cops wouldn't catch me in the act."

Nicole glared at him for a minute, then bent down to look at the snowlike pile of ruined flowers at her feet. "What do you think is going on, Rand?"

He sighed heavily. "I don't know," he replied, crouching down beside her. "But come look at this." He got to his feet, offering Nicole his hand. She didn't take it but followed as he led her over to the cooler. "See?"

She looked around, optimistically noting that some of her stock of cut flowers had survived untouched. "See what? That they didn't finish? Maybe Vin interrupted them."

"At least you're not accusing me anymore."

"Not at the moment, no."

Rand shot her a disgusted glance, then continued. "At my place it was harder to tell, because my inventory is smaller, but it's quite evident here. They had to pick and choose, Nicole."

"What?"

"There's some other stuff thrown in, almost as if to make it look random, but they got all the auratum."

Nicole shrugged. "We had just split the shipment, Rand. The lilies were nearest the door here, probably at your place too."

"Yes, but every last stem? I'm having a very hard time believing it was an accident that they managed to destroy that entire shipment," he told her, arching his eyebrows dramatically. "Think about it."

She was thinking about it. It was the only connection between the two break-ins, unless somebody was going around making mulch out of every florist's shop in town. The police would know. She would ask tomorrow.

Until then, however, Rand's theory made a certain kind of bizarre sense. Some roses had been pulled from the cooler, as well as a few mums and carnations, but every last one of the auratum lilies lay in snowy white tatters on the floor. It did look as if whoever had done this had some design in mind.

Rare, yes. Expensive, definitely. But they were still only imported flowers. "Why?" Nicole wondered aloud.

"Well, the shipment itself was worth a lot of money, and yet it's all too obvious they didn't care about the flowers themselves. And this doesn't look like mindless vandalism. They were too thorough, almost as if they were looking for something. And I say *they* with good reason," he added pointedly. "One person couldn't have done this much damage so quickly."

He was right, she realized, but she countered, "You have employees, too, Rand."

"For heaven's sake, Nicole—"

"Let's drop it. For the moment we'll pretend we're both as innocent as lambs." She turned and walked out of the cooler, deep in thought. It didn't make any sense. "Why didn't they just steal whatever it was they were after and take off?" she wondered aloud, growing more puzzled by the vandals' actions by the moment. "After all, the flowers were all in easy to carry buckets."

"I don't know."

"Wait a minute," Nicole said, her mind slowly shifting into gear. "Were the lilies the only shipment you received today?"

Rand frowned. "No, I got in three different orders." He looked at her, a light dawning in his tired brain. "I get it. Whoever did this wasn't exactly sure what they were looking for or where it was hidden. And the only product you picked up from me today were the auratum lilies."

"That's the connection," she agreed. "But what would someone be looking for in a shipment of cut flowers from the Netherlands?"

"Who knows? Right now I'm not as worried about what they were looking for as whether or not they found it," Rand remarked. "Is this the end of it or can we expect to see them again?"

The roar of the rain had dwindled even further, allowing them to hear another sound echoing across the shipping dock. It was a slow, rhythmic noise, like someone clapping their hands. Rand and Nicole turned and saw a man standing in the doorway, applauding them as if they were players on a stage.

"Very good," he said in a voice made deep and raspy by the foul cigars he smoked, one of which he now held clamped between stained teeth. "I just love to watch amateur detectives in action."

He was wearing a khaki-colored trench coat, and perched at a rakish angle on his head was a sporty green-and-tan checked hat with a narrow brim. The coat, hat, and his beefy shape combined to gave him a look Nicole associated with a football coach standing on the sidelines of a game. His hair was gray, at least what she could see of it, and his face was deeply tanned, with a stubbly gray beard adding to his grizzled appearance.

"Who are you?" she asked.

He reached beneath his coat. Rand stepped protectively in front of Nicole, and the man laughed. Nicole didn't like his laugh. She couldn't decide whether she liked the way Rand was shielding her or not. It wasn't the kind of gesture she'd ever seen anyone do in real life. It made her realize she knew very little about Rand's background.

"Relax, son. I'm a professional."

"Professional what?" Rand muttered.

"Detective," he replied, still chuckling as he withdrew a wallet from an inside pocket, flashing a shiny badge and credentials. "Lieutenant Koslyn. All the patrolmen are out there in the rain, directing traffic around wrecks and downed power lines or investigating reports of lightning strikes." Grinning at them around his smoldering cigar, he put his badge away and stepped farther into the room. "You'll have to make do with me tonight, I'm afraid."

"Lucky us," Nicole said in a low voice so only Rand could hear. He looked at her, his expression telling her he felt the same way. Policeman or not, there was something about him neither of them liked. "You're responding to our call about a break-in?" she asked.

"Unless you two sleuths have already solved the case," he returned with a derisive sneer.

"Look, Detective Koslyn," Rand said brusquely, "if this is beneath you or something, we'd be glad to wait until morning. We're tired and we've had enough unpleasantness for one evening."

Koslyn shrugged, evidently unperturbed by Rand's anger and the insinuation that he was being unpleasant. "As long as I'm here, I might as well look things over." He started wandering around the dock. "From the sound of things I'm not nearly as sharp as you two, but you never know."

They watched as he poked and prodded through the mess, laughing at his own joke. Nicole took Rand's arm, pulling him aside, speaking in a whisper.

"This doesn't feel right, Rand. Shouldn't he be getting our names, writing things down, taking pictures, and stuff like that?"

Rand nodded, watching the lieutenant out of the corner of his eye. "He hasn't even asked what happened. All I told the officer on the phone was that someone had vandalized our warehouses," he whispered back. "And he got here too damn fast, Nicole. You're right. This doesn't feel good at all."

"Well, now," Koslyn said as he came out of the cooler, shutting the door carefully behind him. "Mr. Jameson, Miss Sabine, suppose you tell me what you think these mysterious perpetrators were after?"

"We don't know that they were after anything," Rand answered quickly, giving Nicole's arm a warning squeeze before she could open her mouth. "We were just speculating."

"I see." He stared at them, his brown eyes muddy pools devoid of emotion. "Is anything missing?"

"Not that we know of."

"Have you looked?"

Nicole couldn't stay silent. "What's this all about?" she asked irritably. "Someone broke into Rand's . . . Mr. Jameson's . . . warehouse, destroyed his inventory, then came over here to do the same to mine. It seems to us that somebody has it in for us, but all you're doing is snooping around and making wisecracks."

"Nicole . . ." Rand said quietly, trying to calm her.

"I think you are behaving abominably, Lieutenant," she continued angrily, "and I intend to report this to your superiors."

The man laughed. "What a performance! Both of you, with your who-me attitudes and indignant outrage." He sobered and looked them over thoughtfully. "I don't know, maybe one of you isn't acting. I'd take odds on you, Miss Sabine. Nobody's that good. What about you, Jameson? Care to try your hand at a speech? Threaten me with my superiors, maybe, or a call to your congressman?"

"Spell it out, Koslyn," Rand said in a strange voice that made Nicole turn her head to look at him. "What do you want? A piece of the action?"

"Rand?"

He moved away from her. "Stay out of this, Sabine."

"So," the other man commented dryly, "the wolf takes off his sheep suit at last. That's right, buddy boy. Except I don't want a piece. I want it all."

"That's going to be tougher than you think," Rand told him, his tone calm. He moved to the wall of the shipping department office and leaned against it casually.

Koslyn watched him, his face placid. "You

think so?" he asked. "I've got a gun on my hip and thirty years' experience in pulling it out that says different. Stay where you are and talk fast or you'll see what I mean."

"Hey!" Rand said, raising his hands to shoulder height. "Take it easy. I meant, you're going to have a hard time getting the stuff because I haven't got it. Ask whoever did this." He jerked his chin to indicate the mess on the floor. "I'm as out of luck as you are, friend. We're both too late."

"Would someone tell me what is going on here?" Nicole demanded. "What stuff? Do you know who did this, Rand?" She looked at him, completely bewildered.

"Shut up, lady," Koslyn told her sharply. Then he turned to Rand. "Who do you think you're playing with, Jameson?"

He paused, threw the stub of his cigar on the floor, and crushed it with his foot. Then he opened his coat so they could see the gun he had in a holster clipped to his belt. "Let's get a few things straight right now. I'm holding all the cards here, buddy boy, so I don't mind telling you I don't even know what was in this shipment. But I know it's worth big bucks. And I also know they didn't get it."

"You're sure about that, are you?"

"Yeah. I've been onto this like a tick on a dog from the start. It threw me when you divided the shipment with little Miss Innocent there, but when they showed up and trashed your joint, I figured it out," he said, tapping the side of his nose with his finger. "I haven't been a cop all these years for nothing. You knew somebody had gotten wise to you and split it up to confuse them."

Rand was looking at him warily. "You're pretty well informed, Koslyn," he said, his voice bitter.

"Now you're getting the idea. I got a tip from a friend of mine, see, a guy like me who's hungry and tired of taking orders," the man explained. "He said something was going on with a shipment out of the Netherlands, cut flowers routed through JFK to here. He didn't have the time to find out what, but he knows it's heavy action, so he passed the information on to me."

"So what?" Rand's eyes had narrowed to thin slits. "So you know it arrived. That still doesn't mean—"

"Come on, Jameson," he said with disgust. "I was there, hanging around your place when our destructive friends dropped by. They came out boiling mad, let me tell you. I followed them, and they left here the same way. I know they didn't get the stuff." He reached beneath his coat, glaring at Rand. "But they'll be back, and you're running out of time. Hand over the goods. Now."

Rand looked at him, then turned his gaze to Nicole. "What do you think he'd do if I told him I haven't got the slightest idea what he's talking about?" he asked her, then added in a louder voice, "You don't suppose he'd make a run for the door, do you?"

"What?" Nicole stared at him. How could he wink at her at a time like this? "Have you lost your mind?"

"He's about to lose more than that, lady," Koslyn rasped. "I'm an old-fashioned cop, Jameson. I don't draw my weapon unless I'm going to shoot somebody. Give me what I want before I do."

"All right," Rand said in a defeated voice. "You win." He lowered his hands, sliding one arm around the corner of the wall he was leaning against. The other he extended straight out, pointing a finger at Nicole. "She's got it."

"Are you crazy!" Nicole yelled.

Koslyn's head swiveled to look at her, his eyes wide with surprise. "What—"

Rand fumbled for the main circuit breaker, and the lights went out, throwing the dock into inky blackness. He dashed toward Nicole, working by memory in the dark, practically knocking her over. She screamed, adding her voice to that of Koslyn's as he ordered them to stay where they were. Then came the sound of the big man falling down with a heavy thud as he slipped on the flowers littering the floor.

Rand ignored everything except the dim outline of the open door. Grabbing Nicole's arm, he dragged her out of the building. They were suddenly in the rain, slipping and splashing through the mud as they ran toward a Sabine delivery van. He opened the sliding door on the side, pushed her in, and dived in behind her, scrambling for the driver's seat.

"Keys!" he yelled.

"You despicable, lying—"

"Thank me later," he shot back. "Where are the keys?"

"Behind the sun visor!" Through the windshield of the van Nicole could just make out Koslyn as he dashed out of the building. "Hurry up!"

The engine roared to life. Rand jammed the vehicle in gear and pushed the accelerator to the floor, making the rear wheels spin wildly in the mud. The rogue policeman was looking in their direction, pointing something at them that gleamed in the dim light of the cloud-covered moon. Nicole closed her eyes. The tires finally found a purchase in the muck, and the van lurched forward.

If she hadn't grabbed the dashboard, Nicole would have rolled head over heels to the back of the van. As it was, she almost toppled out of the passenger seat as Rand swung the bouncing, jerking vehicle into a tight, sliding turn. Water and mud sprayed everywhere, a plume of mire jetting from the back wheels, covering Koslyn from head to toe. Temporarily blinded, he covered his face with his arm as Nicole and Rand roared past.

They zipped by the office, gaining speed, passing greenhouse after greenhouse and leaving Koslyn far behind. Then they leapt onto the blacktopped road. The van slid sideways, leaning to one side alarmingly before Rand managed to regain control and point it straight ahead. The buildings of Sabine Wholesale disappeared into the blackness behind them.

"There's a pay phone at the convenience store on the next corner," Nicole announced in a shaky voice.

Rand was still driving like a man possessed. "So?"

"So, we have to call the police!"

"He is the police, remember?"

"But—"

"Listen, you little idiot," Rand told her curtly, "we have no idea what's going on or who might be involved. He may have friends on the force who are dirty too."

Nicole glared at him. Her hands were shaking and her stomach was turning flips. "You're going to get us killed!"

"You've got it backwards, dear. I'm trying to keep us from getting killed. What do you want to do? Call the cops and wait for some of Koslyn's buddies to take us to a nice, quiet spot outside of town?"

"If you'd given him what he wanted, we wouldn't be in this mess," she moaned, pressing her back against the door to get as far away from him as possible. "How dare you include me in your dirty business?"

Rand took his eyes from the road long enough

to frown at her. "What are you talking about? Give him what? What dirty business?"

"Come off it Rand," she bit out disgustedly. "I've heard the stories about people who use the perishable nature of cut flowers to smuggle things quickly through Customs." She wrapped her arms around her queasy stomach. "No wonder you could undercut my prices all the time. The flowers were just a cover for your real business. What is it? Jewels?" She shivered. "Drugs?"

"What on earth! Are you calling me a smuggler?" he roared incredulously.

"How can you deny it!" she roared back. "Boy, you were one cool customer back there, I'll give you that. Calm and collected, working your way over to the circuit breakers, all the while talking shop with that guy." Nicole shivered again. "What kind of man are you, anyway?"

"Are you kidding me? I was scared to death." He held up his hand. It was trembling. "Still am. And if I'd told that guy I didn't know anything about these supposed goods everyone is after, he would have shot us where we stood."

Nicole looked at him. His face was drawn and deathly pale. "Are you trying to tell me you were . . ."

He nodded nervously. "Lying my rear end off, sister. I've heard the stories too. I'd already come to the conclusion there was something a lot more important than lilies in that shipment. When Koslyn showed up, it confirmed my suspicions."

"I don't believe you."

"You'd better believe me," Rand said in an acid tone. "Until we figure this out, all we've got is each other. It's not easy to prove that a cop has gone bad, and if we go to the police, we might just end up walking right into his hands. Customs would be the next best bet, but the same thing might happen. How do we know this friend of Koslyn's who tipped him off isn't a Customs official?"

He was right. Her eyes widened. "All the confusion in New York. Koslyn didn't say his friend *couldn't* find out what was in the shipment. He said he didn't have time. One doesn't just waltz into a Customs holding area." Nicole hugged herself even tighter. She was so confused, she felt she was coming apart at the seams. Should she trust him? Did she have any choice? "Good Lord, Rand. What are we going to do?"

"I don't know yet, Nicole," he replied. The decisive edge had disappeared from his voice. "I just don't know."

He had taken a back road that lead along an area of undeveloped land near the warehouse district. There was very little traffic on it at this hour, and virtually no buildings or street lamps. And yet Rand was slowing down, pulling the van off to the side of the road. She looked at him, alarmed by the unusual expression on his face.

"What's wrong?"

"Nothing," he ground out through clenched teeth as he stopped the van and opened his door. "Stay here, please."

87

"What are you going to do?"

He ran off without answering. The rain had stopped, and some of the cloud cover was lifting, the pale moon overhead illuminating Rand's form. Nicole sighed and closed her eyes. At least there was one thing she could believe in: Rand's fear was every bit as real as hers. The man who had seemed so unnaturally calm and collected earlier had finally realized the risk he had taken and was now standing by the side of the road, breathing deeply to fight off a sudden attack of nerves.

CHAPTER FIVE

"Feeling better?"

"Some."

Nicole gave him a weak smile. "Me too. It's amazing how a few deep breaths of cool night air can make you feel like a new person, isn't it?"

"I'm not a smuggler, Nicole," Rand said.

"All right."

"You don't believe me, do you?"

"Rand, I don't know what to believe anymore." She sighed. It was after one in the morning, but she was wide-awake. Perhaps it was the coffee they had bought at an all-night store a few miles back.

Though all the Sabine vans had a radio to link them with the office, she didn't know who might be listening in, so Nicole had used the pay phone there to call Vin, telling him what had happened and to alert the family that something strange was going on.

That was all. Just something strange. She didn't know what else to say about the mess in which she and Rand had found themselves. She had no idea what was going to happen now, what her part in it would be, or when she would be able to get back to business as usual.

The same thought had occurred to Rand, and he, too, had alerted his top employee to carry on in his absence, as well as keep an eye peeled for trouble.

"Funny," she said. "I was just thinking the other day how nice it would be to get a break from my routine. I guess I got my wish."

"We'll be all right, Nicole," Rand assured her, hoping he sounded more confident than he felt. "First we have to figure out what's going on. Then maybe we can decide where to go for help."

"I know."

Here she was, teamed with a man she knew little about and trusted very little, and there wasn't a single thing she could do about it. Except keep her eyes and ears open. He seemed capable enough, was certainly much quicker on his feet than she was. She knew he probably had saved her life earlier. For the moment, at least, she could do a lot worse than follow his lead.

"What should we do first?" Nicole asked.

"If anyone was following us, we've lost them by now. I'm heading for my warehouse. There's something I want to check out." He pulled off the freeway and onto a frontage road. Water still stood in the drainage ditches on either side, evidence that the storm had hit this part of the city just as hard. "We'll park nearby and sneak in the back way," he informed her. "Just in case Koslyn or the others decided to stake the place out."

Nicole's clothes were now dry and the van's heater pleasantly warm, but she still shivered involuntarily. "I think that's part of my problem, Rand. You seem to be good at this kind of thing. Why?"

"I read a lot."

"Seriously."

"It's true!" he objected. "Haven't you ever read an adventure story or watched a movie and put yourself in the hero or heroine's place?"

Nicole shrugged. "I'm rather addicted to television cop shows myself," she admitted. "And I suppose you're right. Everybody wonders how they'd react under that kind of pressure."

"Now we know," he said with a wry smile. "When real people are confronted with danger, they hyperventilate."

She chuckled in spite of herself. "I'm glad you waited until after you'd gotten us away from Koslyn."

"Oh, I don't know. Maybe it would have convinced him we were innocent. Now he's probably convinced of the opposite, as are the people who tore up our places. Whatever it is everybody's after, we're the ones who supposedly know where it is. We've either got to find it and turn it over to the proper authorities—whoever they may be— or find some way of proving we're not involved."

"Tall order," Nicole commented.

Rand pulled the van onto a side street and

turned off the engine. "Let's go see if we can't start whittling it down to size."

It was dark and very quiet, save for the noise of air-conditioning plants and the pervasive, ever-present hum of a big city. Staying to the shadows between buildings, Rand and Nicole managed to get into his warehouse without anyone seeing them, or at least as far as they knew.

Once inside, Nicole was oddly relieved to see proof that Rand's stock had indeed been given the same thorough treatment as hers; the place was a mess.

"You were right," she said. "They did a better job of it here. Did they leave you anything?"

"That's what I'm here to find out." He looked at her apologetically. "I left in a pretty big hurry, bent on confronting you with your evil deeds."

As at Sabine, all the auratum lilies had been torn to shreds. There were, however, a few bundles of various cut flowers still in water-filled buckets at the very back of Rand's cooler. He went in and sorted through them.

Nicole jumped when he yelled excitedly and came out of the cooler carrying a bunch of gladiola, their thick, dripping stems held together with wide rubber bands. He shook them triumphantly, spraying her with water.

"Hey!"

"Sorry. But here we go," he said, holding the flowers out for her to see. "The only remnant of that shipment."

She frowned. "Glads? What were those doing

92

in that shipment? Most of those come from Florida, California, and right here in Colorado."

"I know," Rand agreed. "And the fact that they're so unexpected is the only reason they survived. When I found them mixed in with the lilies, I thought they'd just gotten packed into the shipment my mistake. Now I'm not so sure." He put them in her hands. "I set them aside, thinking maybe I'd give them to you as a gift. That was before the sky fell on us. I guess it's the thought that counts."

They were beautiful. She stroked their feathery blooms, then touched Rand on the arm. "If they can help us figure this out, I'd say they're the best gift I've ever gotten."

"You know we're going to have to—"

"Tear them up? Yes," she said sadly. "Whatever it is these people are looking for, it's obviously small enough to be concealed in them, or they wouldn't have shredded the auratum."

Rand nodded. "That's what I figure. Ripping up the flowers and the cartons they came in, even throwing the contents of our file cabinets all over, it all points to something very small—and very valuable."

"Like what, do you suppose?"

"I don't have any idea." He cleared off the desk near the cooler and sorted through the mess on the floor until he found a couple of the knives his crew used to open boxes. "It seems unlikely anybody could conceal enough drugs in flower stems or between layers of a cardboard carton to make smuggling them worthwhile."

"Jewels?"

"Maybe. Or papers of some kind, like valuable old documents or some such." He handed her a knife. "Let's get to it."

"Right."

They set to work dissecting the flowers. It was tedious work, since they didn't know how fragile whatever it was might be, or even if there was anything to find in the first place. The vandals hadn't been very delicate in their search, but then, they might have known what they were looking for.

Nicole had just sliced into her fifteenth stem when the blade of her knife hit something hard. She stopped cutting immediately and looked up at Rand.

"I think I've got something."

"Let's see."

Working carefully, Rand slit the thick stem open the rest of the way and pulled from within it a long, slender tube. It looked like the glass pipettes he remembered breaking so many of in his college chemistry days, except that it was thicker and made of a flexible, opaque plastic material. One end was blunt and had been sealed with some sort of rubbery substance; evidently the other had been heated and stretched until it snapped, leaving a sharp point for easy insertion into the flower stem.

"What is it?" Nicole wondered aloud.

"Why are you whispering?"

"It looks so . . ." She stared warily at the tube he held in his hand. "So ominous."

Rand nodded, setting the pipette down on the desk as if afraid to handle it. "Doesn't it, though? I wonder what's inside?"

"Don't open it!" she exclaimed.

"Why not?"

"What if it's some kind of poison or a deadly bacteria or nerve gas or—"

He chuckled, though worry lines creased his forehead. "What an imagination! I guess you do read as much as I do."

"Oh, really? Then why are *you* whispering now?"

"Well . . ." Rand glanced at her and cleared his throat. "I think poison's out. Why smuggle a sample? It would be safer for a courier to memorize the formula, wouldn't it? No customs to worry about that way. The same would be true of nerve gas, and I don't think this plastic tube would be a good place to keep a deadly gas or bacteria, in any case."

"You don't know that, Rand," she returned defiantly. "We have no idea what we're dealing with here. I say we should take it to the police."

Rand was rolling the tube around on the desktop with his fingertip. "And maybe walk right into Koslyn's hands? He'd open it without a second thought, you know."

"I suppose you're right." She frowned thoughtfully. "Then how about a government agency of some kind?"

"I like that idea better," he replied, "except that I'm just cynical enough of the so-called intelligence community to wonder what might happen to us if we try. How do we know who to call?"

Nicole's frown deepened. "What do you mean?"

"Koslyn's a cop. His tipster might be a Customs official. How do we know the people who tore up your place and mine looking for this aren't rogue agents of some kind?" He picked up the tube and held it to the light. "What if we make the wrong choice, Nicole? We could put something very important into the worst possible hands."

"Lord," Nicole said, sighing and rubbing her tired eyes. "As if I didn't have enough responsibility just running a business, someone has to drop this into my lap."

Rand grinned. "And to think I'd be in this alone if you hadn't wrangled a third of that shipment from me."

"Don't remind me." She glared at him, then turned her attention back to the tube. Her mouth dropped open in horror. "Rand! The plug is coming out!"

"Hmm," he hummed, examining it intently. "So it is. Must be the warmth of my hand making the air inside expand. I told you it wouldn't be a good method for smuggling anything dangerous."

Nicole jumped up so fast, the chair she had been sitting in toppled to the floor. "Put it down!" she cried, backing away from the desk.

"Too late."

The plug fell out and bounced on the desktop. Rand peered into the end of the tube. Panic grabbed hold of Nicole's mind and she screamed, making a dash for the cooler and shutting herself inside. The cold air would save her!

Wedging her shoulders into one corner, she took a deep breath and held it, closing her eyes tightly. Poor Rand! She hadn't even had the chance to tell him that she was starting to believe him. She hoped the end would be swift.

Her eyes popped open when Rand staggered into the cooler, clutching his throat and gasping. "Rand! Is it—"

"It's all over," he rasped, clawing at the air. "No danger now. You're safe." He leaned his back against the cooler wall and slowly sank to the floor. His hand waved weakly, motioning her to come closer. "I—I have to know . . ."

"What?" She went to him, sinking to her knees beside him and taking his outstretched hand. He squeezed it and pulled her closer. "What is it, Rand?"

He put his mouth to her ear. "Could we . . . could we have become . . . friends?"

"Yes!" Tears welled in her eyes as she looked at him, cradling his face in her hands. "We could. Oh, Rand! I'm so sorry."

Rand smiled bravely. "Do something for me?"

"Anything!"

"I must know, before I . . ." He coughed. "Kiss me."

Nicole hesitated. His eyes fluttered closed. "Of course," she said, leaning close to him. Her lips touched his lightly. "How was that?" she asked.

"Not bad." Rand pulled her into his lap. "Let's try it again. Only this time, let's pretend you're the one who's dying and I'll give you artificial respiration."

"Damn you!" Outraged, she rolled away from him and stood up, her knee finding his most sensitive area as she did so. He fell over on his side, moaning. "Of all the low, disgusting . . . I could just murder you!"

Rand pushed himself up to a standing position, the distress on his face real now. "I think you just did," he gasped.

"Good! You deserve even worse. I can't believe you did that!" She grabbed one of the buckets he kept his cut flowers in and vindictively poured the chilly water inside over his head. "There! That should cool you off. Kiss me before I die, indeed!"

"I'll catch my death of cold!"

"One can only hope," she returned bitterly.

Leaving him hunched over in the cooler, Nicole strode outside, pacing back and forth until her fury subsided. Then she went to the desk to see what had really been in the mysterious tube. Rand joined her when he had recovered sufficiently, drying his hair off the best he could with some paper napkins he found on the floor.

"I'm sorry," he said. "I guess it really was a pretty lousy thing to do."

Nicole refused to look at him. "You think that fixes everything, don't you?" She pretended to examine the tube, though she hadn't the slightest idea what was inside.

"I just thought it might help if I injected some humor into this mess," Rand shot back irritably.

She glared at him. "Well, it wasn't funny."

"Because you thought I was really dying?"

"Yes!"

Rand smiled at her. "You cared?"

"Of course I cared! I . . ." Nicole trailed off and turned away from him. "Let's forget your stupidity and get back to the matter at hand, shall we?" she asked curtly. "What is this in here?"

He took the tube from her. His wolfish grin vanished as he sat down next to her and said seriously, "You're going to wish you had had a good laugh first, Nicole. It's worse than we thought."

With his hair standing on end from his efforts to dry himself off, he looked rather comical. But his expression didn't make her feel like laughing at all.

"Why? What is it?"

He took a pair of tweezers from the top of the desk and pulled the end of what looked like audio recording tape out of the tube. "It's magnetic tape of some kind. I'm not sure, but I think it's the size they use for storing computer data, or used to use before all the new developments in data-storage technology."

"So? Why does that make the situation any worse than if it had been diamonds or drugs?"

"I suppose it wouldn't be if organized crime was involved, but those guys operate on a grander scale than this, Nicole," he explained. "This would be small-time. And as ruthless as they undoubtedly are, small-time diamond and drug smugglers operate within the law for the most part."

"Sure," she said derisively. "Just everyday folks, right?"

Rand glared at her irritably. He was getting very tired. "I said for the most part. They make their dirty deals and spend their dirty money, but they pretty much walk a straight line otherwise. They have to."

"What are you getting at, Rand?"

"If I'm right, we're dealing with people who can operate above the law, because in a way they are the law," he replied. "I think we've landed smack in the middle of some kind of intelligence operation."

Nicole's eyes widened. "Spies? Government secrets?" she asked incredulously. "Come on, Rand. Now who has the vivid imagination?"

"People store information on this kind of tape, Nicole. With all the trouble someone has gone to getting this into the country, you can bet it isn't a laundry list," Rand told her in a curt, patronizing tone.

"Then what?" she bit back.

"Some sort of technical data would be my guess, since something simple wouldn't require this much intrigue." Picking up the rubber stopper, he forced it back into the tube as if he could contain the danger it represented. "People who deal with stuff like this are capable of doing anything," he said quietly, his expression grave. "And getting away with it. We are in big trouble."

Nicole stared at him for a moment, then at the tube containing the computer tape, her mind struggling against fatigue. This couldn't be happening. That morning, all she had to worry about was making sure Rand didn't shortchange her when they split the shipment.

Now the shipment had been destroyed; Rand was telling her they were very probably in possession of some kind of top-secret material; and there were desperate men lurking somewhere who wanted that material badly. One of them was a cop gone bad. The others could be spies, maybe even rogue agents from her own government, and in Rand's opinion they were very dangerous men indeed.

"I don't think I can stand much more of this, Rand," Nicole said, her voice shaking. She folded her arms on the desktop and rested her head on them. "I'm so tired. I want to go to sleep and wake up to find this has all been a bad dream."

She closed her eyes. A moment passed, and then she felt Rand gently stroking her back, his touch soothing and exciting at the same time. A sigh escaped her lips.

Maybe she should still be mad at him for tricking her into kissing him, but right now she needed comforting, and he was strong enough to give it to her. Nicole needed him. She was too tired and too frightened to question any hidden motives or meanings.

"It is a bad dream," he said softly. "And we'll wake up eventually. It's just going to take time, that's all."

"Oh, Rand." She blew out a deep, sighing breath and raised herself on her elbows, turning to look at him. "What are we going to do?"

He tucked the tube into his shirt pocket and pulled her to her feet. "At the moment we're going to go back to the van, drive to the biggest, brightest, most populated hotel we can find, and get some sleep," he informed her, leading her toward the door. "We're both dead on our feet. We can't make decisions this way." He put his arm around her, felt her warmth as she pressed herself against him. "See what I mean? A little bit ago you wanted to murder me. Now you're hugging me."

"I'm not making a decision, Rand," she informed him sleepily. "I'm just too frazzled to walk by myself, that's all." What a lie! He felt good, his strong arm wrapped around her waist. "Now shut up and get me to a bed."

Rand chuckled. "Anything you say, dear."

CHAPTER SIX

They found a big hotel that was so crowded, they could only get one room—or so Rand said—and that had only a double bed. Nicole didn't bother arguing. By the time they checked in, she could barely keep her eyes open and didn't exactly relish sleeping in a room by herself, in any case.

Even so, she experienced a moment of anxiety when she emerged from the bathroom to find Rand in bed, fast asleep. He had the covers over him, and judging from the neat pile of clothes on a nearby chair, he fully intended to stay right where he was. At least he slept in his briefs, unless he was doing so out of consideration for her modesty.

So much for the gallant offer she had somehow expected him to make: to sleep fully clothed on the floor. In view of the day they'd both had and the fix they were in, she supposed it would be silly to wake him up and demand that he do so. But Nicole wasn't about to sleep on the floor, either, nor was she going to jump into bed in her blouse and skirt. Men had it easy. Let Rand try to sleep in a bra and see how he liked it.

Deciding she could be just as adult about this as he was, she turned off the light, removed all her clothes except her lacy panties, then grabbed his T-shirt from the chair and wore it like a nightgown. Luckily he was a tall man, so it covered her to mid-thigh. She slid in beside him, sighed at the utter ecstasy of being in bed at last, and was soon fast asleep.

Once the exhaustion had been cleansed away by a few hours of blessed oblivion, however, Nicole started to dream. Then the dreams turned to nightmares, full of faceless men with guns, chasing her down dark alleyways littered with crushed, ruined flowers. Trapped in a cul-de-sac, evil advancing upon her like a slithering snake, she tried to move but found her legs paralyzed, opened her mouth to scream, and discovered she was mute.

"Nicole! What's wrong?" Rand grabbed her flailing arms and held her close, as much out of self-defense as to comfort her. "Wake up!"

Gasping, damp with perspiration, Nicole at last escaped the horror within her mind. Her wide-open eyes finally focused upon Rand's face. She was safe, in his arms, in a strange room but far from the black passages of the nightmare. Light streamed through the windows, drawn curtains diffusing it into a soft glow.

"Rand!" She buried her face in his chest,

breath rasping in her throat. "I was being chased, they had me, I couldn't get away—"

"Ssh. It's all right." He stroked her, his fingers caressing her baby-fine blond hair. "You're safe now."

At least she was safe from dreams. Rand wasn't at all sure she was safe from him. Her slender body was pressed against him, the taut muscles of her thighs intertwined with his. Small, firm breasts heaved beneath him as he lay half atop her, comforting her, hard nipples rubbing his chest through the thin, damp material of the shirt she wore. It was his T-shirt, he realized, and somehow the thought pleased him so much that he chuckled throatily.

Nicole lifted her head to look at him, puzzled, her dilated pupils making her seem like a fearful little girl. But she was most definitely a woman, all woman, her parted lips full and inviting. Deep within her pale gray-green eyes Rand could see a delicious emotion stirring. There was a different kind of awakening taking place within her body now, a glow coming to her skin that had nothing at all to do with fear. A slight, almost instinctive adjustment of her hips against his tipped him over the edge.

He kissed her, softly at first, his lips barely brushing hers. Her breath was sweet and warm against his cheek, still ragged, but becoming slower, deeper, now almost a sigh. She moaned softly when his tongue slipped between her lips to fill her mouth, and she met it with her own, a tentative touch that made a wave of heat flow through her.

"Rand . . ."

"Quiet. I'm giving solace," he told her in a soft, teasing voice.

Tracing the round curves of her face, his lips caressed her high cheekbones, her proud jaw, pausing to savor the delicate skin of her throat in passing. Nicole trembled at his touch as his hand wandered beneath the shirt she wore, gliding around the smooth skin of her side to pull her still closer to him.

"I—I'm fine now, Rand. Really."

"You're more than fine," he murmured in a throaty whisper. "You're fantastic. So soft and smooth."

The bed covers were pushed aside, and he lifted the shirt up to her waist, dipping his head to softly kiss her stomach. His teeth nipped delicately at her skin as he raised the thin cotton shirt still higher, caressing her rib cage with his cheek, savoring her womanly scent and the heat of her body.

Nicole moaned, knowing she should stop him but unable to find the will to do so. She needed him, needed this moment of mindless pleasure and the special brand of comfort he was offering her. Soon they would have to face the dangers this day would bring. Until then, they were simply a man and a woman, with no concerns save how to please each other.

"Wait," she whispered, her trembling hands cradling his face as her eyes met his.

"I'm sorry. You're just so beautiful, Nicole. I know I shouldn't take advantage of you—"

Nicole cut him off by putting a finger to his lips. "We're taking advantage of each other, Rand. There's nothing more to it than that," she said, hoping her eyes could communicate words she didn't know how to say. She still had all her doubts. But a more powerful force was burning inside her, pushing aside her caution. "I need you too."

"Nicole . . ."

He found himself unable to continue as he watched her remove the shirt and cast it aside. She was lovely and slender, yet perfectly proportioned, at least in his eyes. Her breasts were compact, firm, their rosy peaks hard with desire. Any doubts she had about her feminine attributes vanished under his appreciative gaze. She leaned back against the pillows with a sigh.

Rand took each of her exquisitely sensitive nipples between his lips in turn, suckling the hard tips, his hands stroking her sides as he buried his face against her. Nicole groaned with pleasure, running her fingers through his thick black hair, liquid fire erupting at the center of her being.

He lifted his head and kissed her, savoring the sweet cavern of her mouth. Nicole's hands wandered freely over him, gliding down his broad, muscled back to his lean hips before moving up along his sides, her fingers exploring the hard, masculine contours of his body. She smiled wickedly, feeling his muscles grow taut beneath her touch. This was solace of the best kind, sensual forgetfulness and passionate comforting.

Capturing his sigh of pleasure with her lips, Nicole then tasted the heated skin of his chest, pausing to look at him slyly as she worked her way down to his hard, flat stomach. He was lean and in good shape; her mind clouded with desire at the thought of what was to come.

"Come on, you little witch," he teased hoarsely, rising from the bed and taking her in his arms. He had to slow things down before he jumped on her, thinking only of his pleasure and unmindful of hers. "Let's see if you're this dangerous when you're wet."

"What's the matter, Rand?" Nicole murmured, nipping softly at his shoulder as he carried her to the shower. "Did I get you too hot?"

He chuckled, amazed by her open sensuality. "Oh, brother. You really do have French blood in your veins, don't you?"

She did, and it was near the boiling point. Suddenly she was standing on the cool tiles of the bathroom floor with Rand right behind her, his thumbs hooked inside the waistband of her panties. As he bent to remove the wispy garment his tongue blazed a path of fire from the base of her spine down her buttocks, along the smooth skin of her thighs. She stepped out of the bit of lace and turned around. Her eyes widened.

He had already removed his briefs. Nicole's

breath caught in her throat at his powerful virility, and she shyly averted her gaze, only to find her eyes returning to him almost immediately. He laughed, hazel eyes sparkling mischievously, then turned to adjust the water running in the shower. Her eyes traced the strong muscles of his calves and thighs, up to his firm, lean buttocks. She fought a blush, but of their own volition her hands caressed his taut, masculine shape, reveling in the way he groaned when she touched him.

Rand stepped into the stinging spray, taking Nicole's hand and pulling her in after him. "So help me, Nicole," he warned as he pressed himself against her, "if you're just teasing me . . ."

"I'm not teasing," she replied, tilting her head to kiss him. Then she laughed, surprised at how hoarse her voice sounded. "At least not in the way you mean."

As if to prove it to him, she grabbed the soap and started lathering his chest, sensuously working her way down along his sides. Rand returned the favor, lingering on her breasts, massaging them until she closed her eyes and had to lean against the side of the shower for support. Then he pulled her to him, his hands lathering and kneading her buttocks rhythmically, the pressure of his hips against hers leaving no doubt in her mind what kind of motion he was suggesting.

Nicole clung to him as they rinsed off, the passion rising within her making her knees weak. His skin felt delicious beneath her fingertips. She wanted him, needed him, right now before she had time to think about what she was doing. Looking into his eyes as they toweled each other off, she wet her lips with her tongue, wanting to communicate her thoughts but unable to force her voice to work any longer.

Rand needed no encouragement. His eyes blazed with desire, his need powerfully evident. He swept her into his arms and carried her to the bed, putting her down gently atop the cool sheets. For a moment he paused, his heated gaze raking over her until she wanted to cry out, then he was beside her, holding her, his tongue plunging into her mouth. Their hearts beat as one, their need equal, urgent hands exploring the wonders of each other's bodies.

Nicole had wanted to forget the situation they were in for a while but had no idea how completely her desire would take over. She writhed beneath him, opening herself to him, meeting his demands with her own. Rand filled her completely, taking total possession of her, his tender power driving her into a mindless, moaning trance.

Never before had Nicole lost control of herself to this extent. It thrilled her beyond reason, yet frightened her at the same time, for in the moment they exploded over the edge together, she felt such an overwhelming need for Rand that she wondered if she ever would be the same.

When she looked at him from now on, would she still see an enemy, a man she couldn't trust? Or would she remember only this moment and find herself wanting him when she should be staying away from him?

But the feeling of having lost some part of herself vanished as quickly as it had come, to be replaced with an inner glow that warmed her to her toes. She rolled atop Rand, moving slowly, gasping with pleasure as he ran his hands along her sides and up to cup her swollen breasts. Nicole clutched at his waist, molding herself to him, the rhythm of their bodies sweeping her away. Her head dipped to his and they kissed, tongues dueling, their every fiber intertwining in a release so powerful, it left them breathless in each other's arms.

They lay together side by side, gently, playfully stroking one another, satiated for now and blanketed in the warm aftermath of their lovemaking. Blessed, much-needed sleep settled in around them at last, and this time they slept without dreaming at all.

It was after noon by the time Nicole and Rand got around to thinking about their predicament again. Well rested and with a room-service meal in their stomachs, they were in a much better frame of mind, full of confidence if still without any cohesive plan.

Their first order of business, they decided, was to get something a little less conspicuous to ride around in than a Sabine delivery van. They also decided Nicole's car would be the safest; Koslyn had been watching Rand, not her. It was a gamble, but they agreed he probably didn't even know where she lived.

She called Jean, the calmest of her two sisters, and asked her to drive the car to Nicole's apartment. Nicole had left it at Sabine last night, and her place was only a few blocks away; but she told her to take the most circuitous route possible. Jean was naturally full of questions but agreed to wait for the answers until they met her there. Just in case, they paid for another night at the hotel, to give them a more-or-less safe haven to fall back on, then took off for Nicole's apartment.

"How do you feel?" Rand asked.

"Fine, considering the mess we're in," Nicole replied, carefully piloting the van through traffic. She had insisted on driving, wanting to keep her mind occupied. Waking up next to Rand had been a pleasant but disturbing experience. What had she done? "How about you?"

He chuckled and put his hand on her thigh. "Great!"

Nicole glanced at him, then returned her eyes to the road. She frowned. "Rand, I meant what I said this morning, before we . . . I told you not to make too much of it."

"What are you talking about?"

"I needed someone to hold me. This all seems so unreal, and I needed a dose of reality." And had she ever gotten it! "Nothing has changed between us," she added, trying to convince herself as well as him.

Rand took his hand from her leg. "I wasn't pledging my undying love for you, Nicole. I needed you the same way."

So he did understand. It was what she had wanted to hear, but why had he said it so angrily? And why did she suddenly feel like crying?

"I just thought it needed saying," she told him, forcing herself to look in his direction again, though she wasn't sure she wanted to see his expression.

He was staring out the passenger-side window. "It didn't. We're both adults."

The remainder of the journey was made in silence. Since it was a new development and the landscaping wasn't mature enough for anyone to hide behind, they were fairly certain no one suspicious was loitering around Nicole's apartment complex when they arrived. They parked the van near her car and went to the front door.

"Nicole!" Jean cried, flinging the door open and hugging her sister before Nicole had even put her key in the lock. "We've all been worried sick. What in heaven's name is going on?"

"Let's discuss it inside, all right?" Rand said, prodding the two women through the doorway.

Once behind the locked door, Jean turned to glare at him. "What have you gotten my sister involved in, Jameson?"

"It's not my—"

"The place was a mess this morning," Jean said, interrupting. "And Vin said a man with a gun chased you both last night. Something about smuggling, he said, and that Jameson was behind it all and . . ." She trailed off, glowering at Rand. "He's laughing at me!" she cried, turning to Nicole for understanding.

Nicole smiled at her. "It's a long story, Jean. Make us some coffee while I change clothes, will you, please? Then we'll tell you what we know."

She decided on blue jeans; a sky-blue cotton blouse in deference to the weather, which was hot and muggy after last night's storm; and a sturdy pair of gray leather tennis shoes. Campus chic, functional yet stylish, and comfortable attire for outrunning bad guys. Nicole hoped she wouldn't get close enough to have to run from anyone, but it didn't hurt to be prepared.

Rand and Jean were eyeing each other warily over the kitchen table when she returned. Coffee was ready, so she poured herself a cup and joined them. Jean, hopelessly addicted to sweets of all kinds, had brought some doughnuts. Nicole took one and ate it, enjoying every bite.

"Well?" her sister demanded.

They told her the story, what they knew as well as what they had surmised, including the nature of the information on the magnetic tape in their possession. Though far from convinced of Rand's innocence—a feeling Nicole admitted sharing, much to Rand's indignant outrage—Jean finally stopped staring at him as if he were some kind of monster.

Then she picked up on the one element of the tale that interested her the most. "You spent the night in a hotel?" she asked, raising her eyebrows. "Together?"

"Jean . . ."

She took one look at Nicole's face and grinned. "If it wasn't for the mess and Vin's eyewitness account, I'd suspect this was something you two cooked up so you could spend the night together."

"For heaven's sake, Jean!" Nicole exclaimed, getting up to get another cup of coffee so her sister couldn't see her flustered expression. Rand didn't help any, sitting there chuckling softly. "This is real!"

"I know." Jean sobered quickly. "The police were by this morning. They didn't know anything about a detective investigating the break-in last night."

"I thought Nicole told Vin not to mention what happened last night," Rand said curtly.

"Don't worry. We played dumb." She sniffed haughtily. "We even pretended we didn't know what was going on when they mentioned they had investigated a similar break-in at your place earlier," Jean informed him. "Not that it was hard. You didn't tell Vin all that much last night, Nicole."

"I know, and I'm sorry," she said. "But I did it for the same reason we hid out in that hotel. I don't want any more of the family involved in this than possible, Jean." Nicole looked at her seriously. "That's why you are going to take the van back to our place, explain what's happening as best you can, and then tell everybody to go on with business as usual. As far as anybody at Sabine knows, I'm on vacation or something. Got that?"

"Sure, but—"

"I gave my employees the same instructions this morning, Jean," Rand told her. "This could be big trouble. We don't want to have to worry about any innocent bystanders getting in harm's way."

Jean nodded, but she wasn't happy. "But you two are innocent bystanders as well." She looked at Rand warily. "At least one of you is, for sure. What on earth do you think you'll be able to do by yourselves?"

"Try to figure out who should get the tape," Nicole explained. "It's all we can do. We're guilty as far as Koslyn, the people who tore up that shipment, and who knows who else is concerned."

"That's right," Rand agreed. "We can't go to the cops because Koslyn might get his hands on us, and we can't go to the FBI or anyone like that until we know who is involved. Our only way out from under is to figure out what's on the tape and get it into the proper hands."

Jean looked dubious. "I suppose that makes sense. But how do you propose to do all this?" she wanted to know. "I mean, you're just a couple of business people. Aren't you in over your heads?"

"Of course we are!" Nicole exclaimed in exasperation. Talking to her sister was making her feel less confident by the moment. She got up, pulled Jean out of her chair, and pushed her toward the door. "Our only advantages are that we managed to find the tape before they did, that they don't know where we are yet, and that we therefore have a chance to get it to the right people before they can stop us."

Jean was dragging her feet. "But why are you doing any of this in the first place? Stop the first one of them you see and give him the damn thing!"

"We can't do that, Jean." Rand got up from the table and assisted Nicole in getting her sister to the door. "We don't know what it is we've got. What if it's defense information or some kind of secret missive intended for our government's eyes only?"

"And what if it's just some half-baked information from one spy to another that nobody but them gives a hoot about?" she asked, trying to pull away from her escorts. "Is that worth putting yourselves in danger for?"

Good question, Nicole thought. But she said, "Just do your part by pretending you haven't seen us, Jean. And don't worry. We're not going to risk our lives." At least she didn't have any plans to do so. She didn't know about Rand. "We're just going to try to do the right thing, that's all. Now get back to work before anybody who might be watching the greenhouses gets suspicious."

They arrived at the door. Nicole opened it, and Rand gently pushed Jean outside. She turned and stood there, looking at them as if they had both taken leave of their senses.

"All right. We'll keep the home fires burning. But let me remind you that the kind of rewards heroes usually get are posthumous!"

"Good-bye, Jean," Nicole and Rand said at the same time.

When they had made sure Jean had left, they returned to the kitchen. Sitting at the table sipping coffee, they looked at each other with grim smiles.

"Just what I needed," Nicole said. "A pep talk."

Rand nodded, chuckling. "Funny. I felt so sure of myself last night. For all we know, whatever is on that tape is important only to the person who sent it and the one who was supposed to receive it. We may be clogging up the works for nothing," he said, obviously annoyed with the whole situation. "What if Jean's right? What if this is just a training exercise for neophyte secret agents? Koslyn's the only one who's threatened us thus far."

"True. And maybe he'd even wander back to the right side of the law if he knew it wasn't drugs or diamonds in the shipment." She reached across the table and took his hand. "We'll just have to muddle through until we know for sure, though, won't we?"

"Yes." He winked at her. "I could do with a

little more comforting just now. How about you?"

Nicole jerked her hand away. "Rand . . ." she warned.

"Just asking, one adult to another," he said irritably. "Go pack a bag in case we can't come back here for a while and let's get going. I'd like to change my clothes, too, you know."

He watched as she disappeared into her bedroom. She was wrong. Whether Nicole was willing to admit it yet or not, Rand knew a lot had changed between them. For one thing, now that he had possessed her, he wasn't about to let it go as some kind of onetime, accidental occurrence. He wanted her, all of her.

There was something else of which he was certain. It was nice to pretend they weren't in any danger and that they could resolve this mess quickly. But deep down he had the feeling that their troubles were just beginning. Perhaps it wasn't the best way to get her into his arms again, but this particular nightmare was far from over. She would need him again, just as she had this morning, and he would be there.

Neither of them would make it through this without the sort of tender comfort and sharing they had enjoyed that morning. Whether Nicole liked it or not, the most bitter of enemies were well on their way to becoming the sweetest of lovers. Rand planned to do everything in his power to speed that process along.

Nicole emerged from her bedroom carrying a

small suitcase. "Ready," she told him, a bit leery of the unusual smile on his face. "You look as if you've figured something out."

"I have." He smiled enigmatically. "I've discovered I have a very forgiving nature. I find myself wanting to thank whoever it was who got me into this mess."

"Thank them?"

He got up, took her suitcase, and led the way out the door. "For making me go shopping," he replied innocently. "We got away with coming here, but I imagine they'll be waiting at my place, so I'll have to buy some new clothes."

"Oh." She laughed nervously, walking ahead of him to open the trunk of her car. "I would think there would be easier ways to get you to buy a new outfit."

"Hmm." Rand admired the gentle sway of her hips as she walked. "Nothing good comes easy."

CHAPTER SEVEN

Shopping with Rand was an enlightening experience. When Nicole went to a mall, she hit every store that carried her size, comparing prices and quality, then took a break and pondered what she had seen. Only then would she make a purchase, and as often as not, she would wait until the items she had chosen went on sale.

Males evidently had an entirely different attitude toward shopping in general. She and Rand chose one of the largest malls in Denver, a glittering, popular place with lots of wide-open spaces that would give them a big crowd to get lost in just in case they were being followed. When Rand informed her that he bought most of his clothes at a shop downtown and therefore didn't know where to go in this place, Nicole had gotten ready for a few hours of pleasant window-shopping. She naturally assumed he would walk around looking for a place that suited his style.

Rand had his own method. First he strode through the mall entrance, walking right up to the massive directory showing the stores and their locations. He then picked a menswear shop at random and took off in that direction, with a purposeful step and nary a glance in any other direction.

"I know we're in a hurry," Nicole said, struggling to keep up with him, "but aren't you going to look around for a little bit?"

"Why?"

Her eyebrows arched at the totally baffled look on his face. "How do you know this place will have what you want?" she asked. Obviously the concept of shopping around was alien to him.

"The directory said it was a men's clothing store," he replied simply.

"So?"

Rand glanced at her as they made their way through the crowd. "I don't follow you," he said, confused.

"You don't know what kind of clothing they sell."

"Yes, I do. I told you. Men's clothes." His tone was impatient. "Pants, shirts, suits. Stuff like that."

Nicole sighed and gave it one last try. "But what *kind* of pants, suits, and shirts?"

"Kind?" He saw the name of the store he was looking for and increased his pace. "I still don't follow you."

"Forget it."

When they entered the store, Nicole realized it was she who was lacking in education. Aside from the occasional tie for her father, cologne for her brother, or a new belt for Vin, she had never really shopped for or with a man. And where her mother, sisters, and she would often go on buying sprees together, it seemed men tended to shop alone.

No wonder so many of them looked like refugees from a bargain basement. They did something no woman in her right mind would do: listened to the advice of the salesperson. It struck her as an incredibly lonely experience for the poor dears. Without a shopping partner, who was going to tell you you looked like a stuffed turkey in this or that outfit?

And Nicole saw that Rand was essentially correct. The shirts, pants, suits, and various accessories on display were in classic styles and colors. Men's clothes. No wonder he didn't bother looking around. Except for the avant-garde places, Rand informed her that the goods for sale were pretty much the same everywhere.

Just as she was about to feel sorry for him for the relatively small options open to a man looking for clothes, however, she remembered how quickly women's clothing went out of style. There was a striking difference in quality too. The slacks he was looking at would last years; she was lucky if the best pair she could find for herself made it through two seasons.

Nicole got even madder when he simply went right to a rack and found what he was looking for. The shirts he bought came wrapped in neat little packages with a size printed on them, a real size in inches instead of some vague approximation. What galled her the most, though, was the way the darn stuff fit him when he put it on. The clothes were designed to look good on men, real, live men.

In the world of women's fashions, if your body didn't have the ideal proportions of a six foot, half-starved model or the lush curves of a buxom starlet, you were out of luck. Tuck it in here, pad yourself out there, and kowtow to the wisdom of the designers.

"This is disgusting," Nicole said bitterly as they left the store. Rand was wearing his new khaki slacks and a short-sleeved shirt of white unbleached linen. The clothes he had on before and his other selections were in a bag slung over his shoulder. "You got a sport coat, two pairs of pants, three shirts, socks, and a snazzy pair of running shoes in less than an hour. It would take me a month to find that much stuff for myself, and then I'd have to take it home and alter it before I could wear it."

"Why?"

She glowered at him. "I hate you. I hate all men. I'm going to run off and become a nun," she vowed. "At least they don't have to worry about what to wear."

"What on earth started that?" Rand muttered under his breath as he watched her stalk off into the crowd.

They got separated for a minute or two, but just as Rand was starting to worry, he found her sitting on a bench near a group of fast-food shops. She was gobbling an immense slice of pizza.

"That looks good."

She handed it to him. "Here. You eat it. It'll probably sink to my hips in five seconds and tear the zipper right out of my jeans."

"What's wrong with you?" Rand asked, sitting beside her. "You have a lovely body. If anything, you could stand a few pounds," he added, giving her back the pizza.

"A lot you know. I'm flat as a pancake and have a bottom like a pear."

Rand put his arm around her. "I have seen both of the areas in question, Nicole, and feel obliged to tell you you're crazy," he informed her, giving her a squeeze. He leaned closer and whispered in her ear. "You have long, beautiful legs, an incredibly sensual rear end, and I haven't been able to get the image of your succulent breasts out of my mind all day."

"Rand!" she objected in a whisper, pushing him away.

"Not to mention another area I've seen for myself and am quite taken with." He winked at her rakishly. "Natural blondes are highly prized, dear."

Spots of color appeared on Nicole's cheeks. She started to get up, but Rand held her arm. At last she looked at him and laughed ruefully. "You're a liar but a sweet one. Thanks."

"Anytime. And every word was the truth."

They shared the rest of the pizza, then stood up and strolled along the storefronts. It all seemed so normal, as if they were simply spending an afternoon shopping like everyone else around them.

Nicole forced herself to break the spell. "What now?" she asked, looking curiously at Rand as he perused the mall directory.

"I'm not sure. I think I'm getting the glimmer of an idea, though," he replied. "I wonder if there's one of those computer stores in this place?"

She pointed at the plastic overlay depicting the shops in numbered, color-coded sequence. "Right there."

"How did you know?"

"My brother's into computers. Most teenagers are these days, I think. He took me there once to show me the latest widgets, trying to convince me to computerize our operation," she explained. "I kind of liked the idea, but Dad didn't, and needless to say, Vin had a fit. Technology isn't one of his favorite subjects."

"Do you think they'd be able to tell us anything about the tape we acquired?" he asked, patting the pocket of his pants where he had the mysterious tube.

Nicole shrugged. "Worth a try, I suppose. Are you even sure it's a computer tape?"

"Pretty sure. It might be some sort of audio or video tape, though. I think it's time we found out, don't you?"

"Definitely. For all we know, it could be a collection of golden oldies or outtakes from some movie."

Rand chuckled, taking her arm and leading the way to the electronics store. "I don't think anyone would go to this much trouble for a Woody Allen film clip, Nicole."

"I guess not. Just wishful thinking."

"It would be kind of funny, though," Rand mused. "Here you go, Detective Koslyn. A rare and valuable Bugs Bunny cartoon."

"I don't think he'd laugh."

"No."

The store had a bewildering array of computer and electronics equipment. Evidently they sold, repaired, and taught people how to use everything from microcomputers to video recording equipment. It seemed the perfect place, and Nicole even remembered the salesman who had helped her and her brother.

"Hello, Mr. Swanson."

"Nicole Sabine, isn't it?" the tall, intelligent-looking older man said when he saw her. "Change your mind about computerizing your flower kingdom?"

She smiled and took his outstretched hand. "No, I'm afraid my father and grandfather prefer to keep things as they are for the time being." She turned to Rand. "Mr. Swanson, this is Rand Jameson. We have a problem we were hoping you could help us with."

The two men shook hands. "Glad to meet you, Mr. Swanson."

"Dave, please. Glad to meet you, Rand." He looked slyly at the couple. "I get thirty dollars an hour for consulting chores. Is it computer-related?"

"We don't really know, Dave," Rand replied, "but of course we'll be happy to pay for your time." He pulled the tube from his pocket, unstoppered it, and showed it to the other man. "An employee of mine left this behind in his desk after he quit," he said, seeing no reason to tell anyone how they had really come by the tape. "I almost threw it out but decided it looked sort of important. If it is, I'll get it back to my former employee."

Dave took the tube, frowning as he withdrew the end of the tape from it with a tiny gripperlike device he pulled out of his shirt pocket.

"Hmm. It does look rather important, doesn't it?"

Rand chuckled. "Of course, if it turns out to be trade secrets he pilfered from me and put down on tape—"

"Now I understand," Dave said, interrupting with a wry smile. "I was wondering why you didn't just call this former employee of yours and ask him what it was." He examined the tape more closely. "What business are you in, Rand?"

"I'm a wholesale florist."

"Oh. Then you wouldn't have the kind of equipment it would take to work with tape this size. Was this man a college student by any chance?"

"Um, I don't think so," Rand hedged. "Why?"

"Well, I can't be positive, but it looks like the sort of tape used to store data for a large computer mainframe."

"A what?" Nicole asked.

"Mainframe. Think of it as the granddaddy of this little fellow here," the man told her, patting the small personal computer sitting on the counter at which they were standing. "Corporate size, like insurance companies and such use. This appears to be a piece of tape from the kind of data storage devices they use."

Rand looked at Nicole and gave her a secretive wink, as if to say "I told you so." She stuck her tongue out at him, then turned back to Dave attentively as he continued. He was too absorbed in the tube and its contents to notice their antics.

"You don't see it that much anymore, of course, what with hard discs and other high-tech storage methods. That's why I thought this former employee might be a college student," the expert explained. "Some schools use mainframes, but with the cost of new data-storage equipment, there are plenty of them still using tape."

"Is there any way to tell what's on it?" Rand asked.

Dave shrugged. "Sure. It's just like any other recording medium. Play it through the right equipment and you get a reproduction of what's on it," he replied, then handed the tube back to

Rand. "Providing it really is what I think it is and it hasn't been damaged by its ride in your pocket, I could tinker around and eventually get a printout."

"Sounds good," Rand said. "Like I said, we'd be glad to pay you to do that for us."

"As tempted as I am to take your money, Rand, I'm afraid you'd be rather disappointed with the results."

Nicole and Rand looked at each other, the triumph disappearing from their faces. "Why is that?" Nicole asked.

"A computer writes information to its storage medium using code. It can be tough enough sometimes to decipher that code when you know what it is. We don't. But let's say your employee was using a standard, not-too-ancient machine and we get a printed copy. In all probability we would still be faced with coded information, in a programming language that could easily be obscure or even unique."

Rand blinked. "Could you run that by me again?"

"Sure," Dave replied, laughing sympathetically. "It's essentially a language problem. If I could figure out what language the computer speaks, I could translate that into symbols I could recognize. But my translation would still be in a foreign language, maybe even one only your former employee knows how to speak."

"In other words," Nicole interjected, her tone bleak, "the only one who can understand what is on this tape is the person who put it on there in the first place."

Dave nodded. "Like I said, it's a good possibility. You could spend a fortune paying me to find out."

A customer had strolled into the store and was looking at some expensive video equipment. Dave Swanson was obviously anxious to go over and sell him something.

"Thanks, Dave," Rand said. "We appreciate the help."

"No problem. If you're still worried about it, there's a group of computer wizards here in town that might do the work for free, just for the challenge." He reached beneath the counter and handed Rand a business card. "But I wouldn't waste my time if I were you. Go ahead and throw the tape away. Stuck in a tube like that, it's probably just a memento from a computer night class your man took."

Nicole smiled, took Rand's arm, and they headed for the door. "Thanks. We'll let you get back to work."

"Come see me when Sabine is ready to step into the twentieth century, Nicole."

"Will do. Good-bye, Dave."

As they walked out of the electronics store gloom settled in around Rand and Nicole like a blanket. The tape was essentially a dead end, at least as far as it being a way out of their predicament was concerned. By the time they got it translated—if it even could be done in the first place—Koslyn or the others would be breathing down their necks.

"Well," Nicole said with a dejected sigh. "I guess that's that."

Rand nodded. "I can't believe I was so dumb as to expect the information on the tape to be easily understood."

"I was just as naïve, Rand. I don't know what I expected. Some kind of message, I suppose." She chuckled in spite of herself. "If lost, please take me to your leader."

Laughing with her, Rand offered his own translation of the tape. "This information is top-secret. Don't read it."

Nicole was so glad they were in this together, she hugged him. She didn't even mind the suggestive look her display of emotion got her. In fact, for some reason she decided not to explore, Rand's playful sensuality lifted her spirits even further.

"I'm hungry," she informed him.

"Again?" he teased.

"I have a very fast metabolism. Besides, I thought you said I could use a few pounds."

Rand put his arm around her waist, his hand softly stroking her stomach as he gave her a knowing leer. "True. And we have to keep up our strength, you know. We may have to dispel each other's bad dreams all night long."

The thought made her nerve endings tingle, but she pretended she didn't know what he meant and headed for the nearest restaurant. Choosing some surprisingly delectable Chinese food and plenty of hot tea to wash it down, they ate heartily and pondered their next move.

"What now?" Nicole asked, nibbling at an egg roll.

"You're asking me? I'm the one who thought up the idea of having the tape printed out, remember? It's your turn to make a fool of yourself."

She patted his hand. "There, there. Don't be too hard on yourself. After all, we did discover that it probably can't be translated."

"I suppose." He smiled at her. "Poor Dave didn't know the half of it. Now that he got me thinking about it, whatever is on that tape is probably in some kind of secret code that even his computer-wizard friends couldn't break."

"Unless they're spies too," Nicole whispered, arching her eyebrows dramatically.

"Don't laugh. If there's one thing this crazy business has convinced me of, it's that anything is possible."

Nicole ordered more tea, then leaned back in her seat, sipping hers and thinking. An odd little smile slowly tugged at the corners of her mouth.

"It worked last night on my shipping dock," she muttered under her breath. "Why wouldn't it work again?"

"Why wouldn't what work again?"

"Thinking like a character out of a book or movie," she replied. She put her elbows on the table and looked at him seriously. "Let's face it,

Rand. We're about as amateur at this sort of thing as we can be. We have to start thinking like the heroes of some adventure tale."

Rand's expression turned doubtful. "But—"

"You did it last night," she reminded him. "That wasn't really you talking to Koslyn so calmly while scheming to get us out of there."

"It sure felt like me. Especially later, when I had a chance to think about what I'd done."

Nicole waved his comment aside. "No, I mean that it wasn't something you thought of all by yourself. You'd read it in a book or seen it on television or something, right?"

"Right, but I still—"

"So let's do that again," she said, interrupting. "Let's pretend we really know what we're doing."

"That," Rand told her, "will take one heck of a lot of imagination."

She shrugged. "Not really. For instance, I think I already know what a detective would do in our shoes."

"Get into another line of work?"

Nicole ignored him, intent upon her idea. "For starters, let's lay it all out like they do in the movies," she said. "We have some goods that belong to somebody else. We don't know what those goods are or who we should give them to, but we know they're important. There are some people who seem to know more about what's going on than we do, but we haven't seen them as yet."

"So far all you've done is paint yourself into a

134

corner, Detective Sabine," Rand said with a chuckle.

"Would you be serious for a moment?" She glared at him. He shrugged and motioned for her to proceed. "That's better. Now, try to think like a fictional detective. What else do we know, Sam?"

"Sam?"

"Sam Spade."

Rand laughed, then hunched his shoulders. "We know there's a rogue cop after us, sweetheart," he said raspily.

"Right! In fact, other than the things I just listed, that's the only other thing we know for sure. Koslyn's after us."

Rand looked at her, obviously perturbed with her logic. "But he doesn't know what's going on, either, Nicole. He thinks we've got something he can make a profit on. But whatever it is on this tape, he's more likely to get himself killed trying to sell it than anything else."

"Right again!" Nicole exclaimed. "But he would try, anyway, wouldn't he?"

"I suppose he would."

"You know he would. He's greedy, he carries a gun he seems quite willing to use, and he's also got a bit more experience dealing with danger than we do. And," she added, leaning closer and grinning from ear to ear, "he knows something we don't, Rand."

"What?"

"He knows what the people who broke into

your place and mine look like. He was watching them, remember?" she asked, her face flushed with excitement. "As a matter of fact, it may have been his plan all along to grab the goods and sell them back to the fat man."

Rand frowned at her. "What fat man?"

"Oops! Sorry." Her face reddened a bit more. "I got carried away with my character. I mean that even though he didn't know what was in the shipment, he was already planning to take it away from us and sell it to the people who came looking for it," she explained. "If he had the tape, he wouldn't care about what was on it, just about who wanted it and how much they were willing to pay for it."

"So?"

"So we help him."

His eyes narrowed. "Excuse me?"

"It's elementary," she informed him in a dignified voice. "We take it a step at a time. First we turn the tables: stop being the watched and become the watchers. Then we trick Lieutenant Koslyn into thinking he has accomplished his task. He shall lead us to the vandals, who, one hopes, shall in turn lead us to a way out of our predicament."

Now Rand started grinning. "You know, Holmes, it might just work. But it will be bloody dangerous."

"It's already dangerous," Nicole pointed out. "And personally I'd rather be pretending I was someone else, anyway. It seems much less real. I'm tired of being frightened."

"There's just one thing."

"What?"

Rand took her hand and squeezed it. "If it's at all possible, can I have Nicole back soon? I'm growing quite fond of her."

Lowering her eyes, Nicole smiled a secretive smile. "I think that can be arranged. She's getting a little bit fond of you too."

"Just a little bit?"

Nicole looked up at him. "What detective worth her salt would trust anyone completely?"

"What now?" Rand groaned.

"You could be a spy for all I know. Maybe you know what's on the tape. Maybe this is all a ruse you cooked up to confuse the opposition and you're just biding your time until you can dump me and take it to your superiors."

He let go of her hand and stared at her incredulously. "I don't believe this! You're letting that imagination of yours run away with you again, Nicole."

"A good spy would play his role to the hilt. He'd deny my accusations too." She was teasing him in a way, but in a way she was deadly serious. "As you said earlier, Rand, this business is crazy enough to convince me that anything is possible."

"All right," Rand shot back irritably. "As long as we're on the subject, I have a few doubts about you, dear. For instance, I find it rather suspicious that you knew about this shipment from the beginning. And the tricky way you got me to split it with you isn't comforting, either." He glared at her. "How do I know *you* aren't a spy? You dealt yourself into this game pretty handily, Nicole."

"I explained all that."

"So you did," he returned with a sour smile. "A good spy would do a convincing job of that, wouldn't she?"

They faced each other across the table, eyes locked, neither of them blinking. The suspicions between them were real, and they wouldn't be dispelled easily. But since they had no one to trust but each other, they had to make a mockery of their mutual doubts.

Rand's expression softened. "No matter what's going on in that pretty head of yours, Nicole, you've got to believe me. I would never do anything to hurt you."

"Nor I you," she told him, taking his hand. "We have to believe in something or we'll go insane. Shall we make that our common ground?"

He lifted her hand and kissed it softly. "Yes. Come what may, we're in this together. I'll look out for you if you look out for me. I promise."

Nicole nodded. "Promise."

"Now that the two international spies have made their secret pact," Rand said dramatically, "they had better get a move on and start rounding up their supplies."

Laughing with him, she stood up and linked

her arm through his. "Right. What does one need to get an advantage on the competition?"

"I haven't the slightest idea," he replied. "Let's wing it. We already have our most important tools."

"And those are?"

"Our credit cards, naturally. The mall awaits!"

"What do you think?" Nicole asked, holding up a slinky black pantsuit. "Just what the fashion-conscious night stalker needs, right?"

Rand chuckled, nodding appreciatively. "It's you. We'll make a striking couple, you in your cat-burglar suit and me in my black jeans and leather jacket."

"Crepe-soled shoes!" she exclaimed, snapping her fingers. "For creeping up on bad guys!"

"Next stop, a shoe store," he agreed.

Nicole bought a stylish black hat to go with her pantsuit. Rand wanted a hat, too, but she convinced him he didn't need one since his coal-colored hair wouldn't stand out like her blond tresses. In fact, she just thought he looked ridiculous in the felt cowboy hat he tried on.

To console himself Rand shopped for the pair of binoculars he'd always wanted. "Hmm," he hummed, using them to look out the store window at the people passing by. "This is a nice pair."

Nicole followed his gaze. He was focused on a lithe young woman in shorts and halter top sauntering down the esplanade. "Pair of what?" she asked derisively, poking him in the ribs.

"Ouch! We'll need them," he objected.

"All right. Just make sure you point them in the right direction."

"Jealous?"

Nicole put her nose in the air. "Wouldn't you like to know?" she asked airily, then walked away.

Chuckling wickedly, Rand focused the strong lenses on her derriere. "I'll take them," he told the bewildered clerk.

They added to their surveillance gear a telephoto lens for Nicole's camera, as well as some high-speed film the man in the camera shop said they could use in almost nonexistent light. The most amazing item of all, however, was a small tape recorder with a powerful directional microphone, a device that would allow them to record conversations from a safe distance without being observed.

Thus outfitted, they lugged their purchases out to the car, an unwieldy trip that made them go back into the mall for one last item: a black canvas bag with a shoulder strap in which to carry everything. Tired but full of enthusiasm, they then headed back to Nicole's apartment.

There still didn't appear to be anyone following them, nor did their fears of being ambushed in the parking lot of Nicole's apartment materialize. The apartment itself was just as they'd left it. Rather than make them feel safe, however, the seeming lack of interest in them only made them more wary and confused.

A quick call to Jean confirmed at least one suspicion, however. Sabine had had some unusual visitors today: three men who claimed to be real-estate developers whom Vin ran off with glee; and a woman who said she was doing a story on local growers but who seemed more interested in their trash bins than their greenhouses.

There also had been a call from Koslyn. Jean had feigned ignorance. Koslyn had quietly stated he would be waiting. That was all, just waiting.

"They don't seem as desperate as I thought they'd be," Nicole commented when she had finished reassuring Jean and hung up the phone.

Rand had been listening on another line. "No, but that doesn't mean we're safe. In fact, it may mean Koslyn and the others are so well connected, they would know the moment we tried to turn the tape over to someone in authority."

"Depressing thought."

"It makes it even more imperative that we carry out our plans, that's for sure. We have to know how many players are in this game and what their affiliations are."

While Rand fiddled with each of their new gadgets before packing it carefully away in the tote bag, Nicole mixed them some cooling, fortifying frozen margaritas. It promised to be a hot night, in more ways than one.

"Ready?" Nicole asked.

"Ready." They touched glasses in a toast. "Here's to you, Miss Moneypenny," Rand said.

"Excuse me?"

He shrugged. "Seemed appropriate, somehow. Are you going to make the call or shall I?"

"Allow me." Nicole picked up the phone and dialed. "Yes," she said when a gruff male voice answered. "I'd like to speak with Lieutenant Koslyn, please. My name?" She looked at Rand and grinned. "My name is Bond. Jayne Bond."

CHAPTER EIGHT

Full night had descended upon the deserted streets of the warehouse district. The crescent moon overhead was playing hide-and-seek with a large, fluffy cloud scudding across the black velvet sky, its pale, diffused light casting an eerie glow on the city. Somewhere amid the maze of buildings and asphalt an alley cat yowled his challenge to a rival. The business day was over; now was the time the animals came out to play.

"Lower and to the left."

Nicole moved in the darkness, laughing quietly as Rand moaned and groaned beneath her. Her fingertips probed him, feeling his muscles grow taut at her delicate touch.

"There?" she whispered.

Rand moaned again. "Oh. Yes. You have such strong, wonderful hands, Nicole."

"I play in the dirt a lot."

"Sounds intriguing."

"You faker!" She took her hat off and hit him playfully on the back of the head with it, rolling off him and out of his reach. "How dare you pretend to be in agony?"

"You cured me." With a wicked chuckle he scrambled across the rooftop on his hands and knees, grabbing her ankle to keep her from getting away. "Now it's my turn."

"Ssh!"

Rand pinned her legs beneath his, cradling her head in the crook of his arm. "I won't make any noise if you won't," he informed her in a hushed tone.

He pulled the zipper on her pantsuit down to her stomach and slipped his hand beneath the silky black material, caressing the soft tips of her breasts until her nipples hardened beneath his palm. He lowered his head and plunged his tongue into her mouth to silence her moan of pleasure.

"Stop that," she murmured halfheartedly.

"Ssh!"

"I thought you'd strained your back."

"I did. I don't regularly climb up the sides of buildings, you know. But I'm fine now." He grinned, his teeth white in the dim light. "Besides, my hands are fine. See?"

Nicole groaned as he massaged her breasts. "Y-yes, I can tell your hands are just fine." She pushed him away. "Now use them to zip me back up. Koslyn could get here any minute."

"We're way ahead of schedule," Rand objected.

"If we thought of coming early, so will he."

Rand sighed. "All right." He dipped his head to kiss her lightly on the belly, then pulled her zipper back up to her neck. "I just got carried away by all the excitement."

"They say adrenaline can be a powerful aphrodisiac," Nicole said. She smiled and pressed her lips to his. "And they're right. I'm not immune. We just have to keep our wits about us."

"Agreed. But later—"

Nicole laughed throatily. "Agreed."

They crawled back across the roof, its flat tin surface still warm from baking under the sun all day. At the rim was a wall of brick about three feet high. They crouched behind it, looking down on the street below. The things they had bought at the mall earlier were in the black canvas bag at their feet.

Directly across from them was Rand's warehouse, all the windows dark except the one looking into his office. It was risky using this place, but they needed a spot they had easy access to in order to set things up for this meeting, as well as one from which they could observe Rand's office from a distance. And since Rand's employees had been visited that morning by some bogus real-estate agents and a trash-inspecting reporter, just as Sabine had, they figured the heat was off for the time being.

Evidently they were right. Unless they were being watched by someone who was very sneaky—a possibility they didn't rule out by any means—it seemed that they and the beasts of the night were the only ones stirring in this moonlit concrete jungle.

"Hand me the binoculars," Rand whispered.

"Is there a pretty girl walking by?"

He looked at her with a wounded expression. "I had to make sure they worked, didn't I?"

"Here. Stick them in your ear."

"I wouldn't be able to see anything that way." He lifted the binoculars to his eyes, peering down at the streets. "Rats."

"What's wrong?"

"Nothing's wrong. That's what I see. Rats."

"Yuck! Keep that kind of observation to yourself," she said, looking around the rooftop warily and scooting closer to him. "Now you've got me thinking there are a hundred beady little eyes looking at me right this minute."

"Let's just hope they're all rodents and not rats of another kind," Rand murmured.

Nicole shivered, though the night air was soft and warm. "You can keep that kind of talk to yourself too," she informed him. "Can you see into the office?"

"Perfectly. Do you want to see?"

"I'll use this." She lifted her camera out of the bag and focused the telephoto lens on the office window. Rand's desk came into view. Like a spotlight, the lamp atop it illuminated the items they had placed there earlier. "I hope your idea to check the range of the microphone works."

"It will. And even if it doesn't, we can record him using the walkie-talkies. Let's try it out."

Grinning like a child with a new toy, Rand took the little tape recorder out of the bag, turned it on, and pointed the directional microphone at the office window. He stuck the tiny foam pad of the earphone into his ear, listening intently for a moment and nodding. Then he picked up the walkie-talkie at his side and thumbed the transmit button, holding it up to Nicole's mouth.

"Say something."

"Like what?"

"It doesn't matter. But keep your voice down. This thing's so powerful, I swear I can hear a mouse making a nest in my desk drawer."

"Mice and rats. You need to move to a new neighborhood, Rand," she informed him.

"I heard that!"

Nicole wasn't impressed. "Of course you did. I'm right next to you."

He handed her the walkie-talkie and pointed across the roof. "Go over there and try it again."

"Well, okay," she agreed reluctantly, squinting into the deep shadows surrounding them. "But if something eats me, it'll be on your head."

"Not a chance. I've got dibs on every bite of you."

Crouching low, Nicole tiptoed into the darkness, stopping when she felt she was out of earshot. She thought for a moment, giggled, then whispered into the hand-held radio.

"Rand Jameson has the cutest mole. It's shaped like a little rabbit, and it's right on his—"

A pebble bounced off the roof near her foot.

147

"That'll be enough of that!" Rand called softly. "Get *your* cute little rear end back over here."

"You said I could say anything I wanted," she said teasingly when she rejoined him at the edge of the roof.

"Pipe down and rewind that tape. If we do get something the authorities can use, I don't want them hearing that!"

Nicole fiddled with the recorder. "There. I think that's got it. Do you want it on?"

"Not until Koslyn gets here." Once again he propped the amazing microphone on the brick wall so it was pointing down at the office window, ready to catch Koslyn's every word, then picked up the binoculars again. "Uh-oh. Turn it on. I think he's here, and an hour early, the fink."

"I told you so!" she exclaimed, her heart thumping in her chest. A moment ago this had seemed a great lark. Now she felt her stomach churn. "I think I'm going to be sick."

"Ssh!"

On the street below, a police cruiser was coming slowly down the block. It pulled up in front of the warehouse and stopped, the sound of its idling motor seeming unnaturally loud to the watchers on the roof. Then the driver cut the engine off. Still no one got out. The dim light of the street lamps reflected off the windshield, making it all but impossible to see inside.

"Is it him?" Nicole whispered.

"It must be. What's he waiting for?"

Then a light flared in the cruiser. Someone had

struck a match. The light went out, leaving only a dot of glowing red in the darkened interior of the car. The door opened.

"It's Koslyn," Rand confirmed, watching through the binoculars as the beefy man got out and slowly turned in a circle, checking out the lay of the land.

Nicole crinkled her nose. "You don't have to tell me. I can smell that cigar from here."

Koslyn hadn't been surprised to hear from them. In fact, he evidently considered himself such a threatening individual that he was quite put out with them for not contacting him sooner. Some of that annoyance showed on his face now as he stepped away from the car and slowly made his way to the front door of Rand's office.

His watchers noticed his irritation, as well as the hand he had stuck inside his coat, a strong, tough hand that without a doubt was resting on the butt of his gun. Koslyn might be cocky, but he wasn't stupid. As a matter of fact, his every move, from the way he balanced on the balls of his feet as he walked to his alert, constant scrutiny of the darkened buildings around him, gave them all the proof they needed that this was an experienced police officer. A dangerous man.

Rand muttered a quiet expletive. "Come on, get in there, you—"

"Let's forget the whole thing and get out of here, Rand," Nicole said in a whisper, interrupting him.

"We can't." He touched her shoulder. "Think

149

brave thoughts. You're a rough-and-tumble lady detective, Nicole, remember?"

She swallowed thickly. "That's the problem. All the role models I can think of wouldn't be in this mess in the first place."

"I, myself, am having a hard time conjuring up the image of Sam Spade without a gat."

"A what?"

"Gat. Piece. You know, a gun."

"Do you own one?"

"Well, yes, as a matter of fact I do."

Nicole grabbed his arm. "Then why in heaven's name didn't you bring it?"

Wincing, Rand pried her fingers off his arm. Physically and mentally she was a strong woman but quite obviously scared. She was not alone.

"I haven't been to my house since this started, remember? And, in any case, shooting a paper target is one heck of a lot different from shooting a human being."

"But—"

"This was your idea, Nicole," he reminded her, his own nervousness making his voice crisp. "And it's a good one. Now make sure the recorder is running and get your camera ready. He'll be in the office in a moment."

A loud bang made them both jump. Rand yanked the earphone out of his ear. "Damn!"

"What was that?"

"He kicked my door in!" Rand said, indignant. "Turn down the volume and unplug this thing."

He cast the earphone aside. "We'll listen through the speaker."

Nicole did so, noticing that her hands were shaking. "Now I have to go to the bathroom," she muttered miserably.

"What's going on here?" Koslyn asked. His angry voice sounded tinny through the recorder's little speaker. "I'm through playing with you two. Come out of hiding now or you'll get hurt."

Lifting her camera, Nicole snapped the shutter as Koslyn drew his revolver. She caught another of his face as he looked around the room, a murderous gleam in his muddy brown eyes. But what she imagined would be the best shot of the night was the look of startled surprise on his face when Rand spoke to him via the walkie-talkie.

"Hello, Koslyn."

"What the—" He stepped over to Rand's desk, his expression incredulous.

"You didn't seriously expect us to meet you face-to-face, did you?" Rand asked. "We can hear you and see your every move, Koslyn. Unless you plan to shoot the radio, why don't you put that gun away?"

Koslyn's face turned red with rage. "You call this bargaining in good faith, Jameson?"

"What about you?" Rand returned with a derisive laugh. "I thought you didn't draw your gun unless you were going to use it."

He put the gun back in his holster, then moved to the window, peering out into the darkness at the rooftops. Rand and Nicole ducked down, though they already had made sure their vantage point couldn't be seen from the office.

"Say," Koslyn muttered suspiciously, "what are you guys? If you're with Internal Affairs, so help me . . ." He trailed off and shook his fist at the unseen observers. "This is entrapment. You'll never make it stick."

Nicole grabbed the radio from Rand. "Shut up, you big tub of lard. We're calling the shots now."

Koslyn cursed. Rand took back the walkie-talkie, grinning at Nicole. "Feel better now?"

"Much."

The man in the window across the street was shaking his head and muttering epithets. "Oh, brother. This is cute. Real cute. I knew nobody could be as stupid as you two acted."

"I don't know whether we've just been complimented or insulted," Nicole commented dryly. "But I think we've got his attention."

"You've got the room bugged, right?" Koslyn asked.

"No. We've got that walkie-talkie on the desk on an open circuit," Rand lied. He smiled. It was all part of the plan, to make Koslyn think this conversation wasn't being recorded. "Nice and private. Now go to the desk."

He did so, very cautiously. "What's this thing?"

Through the binoculars Rand watched him gently prod the plastic tube on the desk with his fingertip. "That's what you're here for, Koslyn."

"I don't get it."

Nicole snapped a picture of him picking up the tube and studying it. "You will," she mumbled.

"Pull that little stopper out," Rand ordered, "and take a look at what's inside. Use the tweezers on the desk." The sound of the camera confirmed that Nicole got a shot of him doing so.

"I repeat. What is it?" the other man asked, confused.

"That tape is what was smuggled into this country with the flower shipment, Koslyn. No jewels or drugs. Sorry."

Koslyn turned his face to the window. "What are you trying to pull? My friend said whatever was in the shipment was worth big bucks."

The moment of truth had passed. The rogue detective was as in the dark about all of this as they were. But now came the tricky part. Would he live up—or rather, down—to their impression of him as a despicable, greedy individual, or would he simply call it a day and leave them in a worse fix than they were in now?

"Care to do the honors?" Rand asked, offering the walkie-talkie to Nicole.

She smiled. Her stomach had settled, and the thrill was under control. While Rand took his turn at clicking off strategic photos, she took hers at talking to Koslyn.

"Listen to me, Koslyn," she said firmly but quietly.

"Well. Hello, Little Miss Innocent. Have any other names you'd like to call me while you're safely cowering on some rooftop?"

"I said *listen!*" she shot back. "As you can see, we're not stupid. But whether you believe it or not, we had nothing to do with bringing that tape into the country. Nor do we want anything to do with it now that it's here."

Koslyn laughed derisively. "Sure. Tell me another fairy tale, Sabine."

"What we would really like is for you to pretend you're the public servant you're supposed to be and get that tape to the proper authorities."

Rand grabbed her arm. "Nicole!"

She put her hand on his. "We have to give him a chance, Rand. It has to be his decision."

"You're right." He released her with a resigned sigh.

Nicole picked up the binoculars. From the look on Koslyn's face Rand had nothing to worry about. Earlier his eyes had gleamed with fury; now they held an entirely different sort of sparkle.

"What's on it?" Koslyn asked, holding the tube containing the tape up to the light.

"We don't know. We do know it's a computer tape of some kind, a tape somebody has gone to a lot of trouble to smuggle into the United States from Europe. Figure it out for yourself."

"Spooks," Koslyn said, his voice scarcely more than a whisper. "Spies. Whoever was supposed to receive it, they dropped the ball." He grinned, clutching the tube in his big hand. "And look who it bounced to!"

His voice contained pure greed. It was a disap-

154

pointment in a way but, then again, nothing more than Nicole had expected from him. It had been worth a try, though. Had there been an honest bone in his body, this whole ordeal already would have been over.

"I don't suppose you're at all interested in getting it back into the proper hands?" she asked him, already knowing his answer.

He laughed. "Are you kidding? Do you have any idea what this is?"

"We think it might be intelligence information. It may even belong to our government."

"Who cares?" Koslyn was practically beside himself with joy. "I'll tell you what it is. It's a gold mine, that's what. And it's all—" Suddenly he stopped smiling. He backed away from the window and pulled his revolver. "Now I understand this weird setup. You've got a rifle on me, don't you, Jameson? Just in case I wasn't as patriotic as you two fools."

"Bang," Rand whispered as he shot a picture of Koslyn's grotesque sneer. "Got him."

"You're wrong, Koslyn," Nicole said mildly. "We're not stupid, remember? As much as we would like to, we know we can't do anything to you. No matter what we said, it would look like we were the bad guys, interfering with an officer of the law. You've probably got friends in high places."

Koslyn relaxed a little. "Yeah. You bet I do."

"We took a gamble you would do the right thing. We lost. It was worth a try, but that wasn't

155

what we wanted out of this deal in the first place," she informed him, crossing her fingers.

"Yeah?" He holstered his gun but edged away from the window and out of the line of fire. "What do you want?"

"Out," Nicole replied. "You've got the tape. Go ahead and do what you want with it. In return for our silence on the matter we want out of this mess—and you off our backs."

The sensitive microphone of the tape recorder picked up the sound of his breathing as he considered what she had said. At last, with a bravado that would have been admirable under other circumstances, he stepped closer to the window. He was smiling but cautious.

"How do I know you're on the level?"

It wasn't hard for Nicole to sound honest when she told him, "We're in over our heads, Koslyn. You know how to deal with the kind of people that ransacked our businesses. We don't. We'd like to see that tape in the hands of the proper authorities, but we could get hurt trying to get it there, so we're washing our hands of it. All we want is to be left alone."

"Yeah. That makes sense," he mumbled.

"Is it a deal?"

There was another long pause. "All right. You're off the hook." His smile broadened, and he added in an officious voice, "You've done the right thing, Miss Sabine, Mr. Jameson. I'll handle things from here on out."

"Now I really am sick to my stomach," Rand whispered.

Nicole nodded. There were few things worse than a traitor. "There's just one thing. If anyone pressures us, we're going to tell them we found something odd in the shipment, called the police, and gave it to a Lieutenant Koslyn," she informed him. "We won't take any heat for you. It's in your lap now. We're through."

He chuckled. "I knew there had to be a catch. Okay. I'll get all the gain, so I'll take all the risks," he said, straightening his bulky form proudly. "I can handle it. But if you ever say anything about this meeting"—he patted the butt of his gun—"you'll regret it."

"Who would believe us?" Nicole asked with a grin. The tape recorder whirred nearby, joined by the sound of a clicking camera shutter. "Goodbye, Koslyn."

"So long, suckers. Been nice doing business with you."

He tipped his hat, turned, and left the office, emerging from the building a few moments later. Whistling and puffing merrily on his foul cigar, he climbed into the squad car and pulled away at a leisurely pace.

Once he was gone, Nicole and Rand hurriedly packed up their equipment and climbed back down the fire escape. They retrieved the other walkie-talkie from the warehouse office, then headed for the dark side street where they had parked Nicole's car.

"We did it!" Excitement flowed through her veins like a potent elixir. "And I don't even feel sick anymore."

Rand's step was just as lively as he walked along beside her. "Neither do I. I guess you must get used to it or something. But it's far from over," he reminded her. "Getting him to take the bait was just the first step."

"In a way I guess we told him the truth," Nicole said. "It's his problem now. All we have to do is watch."

They climbed into the car. The radio under the dashboard squawked the moment she turned it on. "Red Rose, this is Orchid. Do you read me? Over."

Nicole broke out laughing, then finally managed to reply. "Loud and clear, Orchid. Go ahead." A stream of French flowed from the speaker. *"Oui,"* she said when it stopped. "And after that, go get some sleep, Orchid. Out."

"How did you get Vin to touch a radio?" Rand asked. "I thought he abhorred technology."

"Not all technology. He's been a ham operator for years. In fact, he was the one who insisted on putting radios in all our cars and delivery vans."

"Good thing too. He spotted Koslyn?"

She nodded. "Heading south. He'll keep him in sight until we can get there and take over, then head on home," she explained. "Hopefully."

"I'm still not so sure it was a good idea to include him in this," Rand agreed.

"We didn't have any choice. Vin had already

wormed most of it out of Jean, anyway. And without him we might have lost Koslyn's trail."

Nicole started the car and pulled out of the alley, doing her best not to speed. All they needed now was to be stopped for a traffic violation. Dressed in black, dusty from crawling around on the roof, and with surveillance equipment in the backseat, they made a suspicious-looking pair indeed.

"I wonder if he'll take the tape to them right away?"

Rand frowned. "I doubt it. He'll probably hide it somewhere and then set up a meeting with them to talk over the price."

"You're right." Nicole laughed. "You must watch the same television cop shows I do."

"The tricky part always comes after the commercial, when the price has been set and they make the switch."

Nicole pulled onto the frontage road and increased her speed, scanning the traffic ahead of her for any sign of Vin's beat-up old truck. "It's the trickiest part of our plan, that's for sure. If they discover too soon that the tape we gave Koslyn is a fake . . ."

"We'll be in a fix if they do," Rand agreed. "I'm hoping they're just pickup men. That way we can follow them to whoever sent them, and so on down the line. As for Koslyn . . . well, you gave him a chance to do the right thing. We'll just have to wait and see what happens."

"Poor Koslyn." She glanced at Rand. He was

grinning. She realized she was too. "Whatever happens, it couldn't happen to a nicer guy."

The radio squawked urgently. "Red Rose, this is Orchid."

"Go ahead, Orchid."

"Something has gone wrong."

"What is it, Vin?" Nicole asked, discarding the code name they had decided to use in case Koslyn had been scanning the civilian frequencies. "Have you lost him?"

"No. I am parked a block behind him."

"Parked? What is he doing?"

"He is yelling a great deal. Three men in a blue car forced him off the road, put manacles on his wrists and are presently trying to shove him into the backseat of their car."

Nicole looked at Rand, her knuckles white as she gripped the radio microphone. "What? Who are they, Vin? Are they policemen?"

"They have on nice suits. One of them is watching me suspiciously, Nicole. He is walking this way."

Nicole was having trouble keeping her eyes on the road. Rand grabbed the microphone from her. "Get out of there, Orchid," he ordered. "Right now."

"Very well, Toadstool. I am leaving now."

Rand shot Nicole a perturbed glance. "Toadstool?"

"Vin's idea." She pointed out the windshield. "Look. There they are. They don't look like the police to me, Rand."

The three men in gray suits had succeeded in getting Koslyn into the backseat of their car. One of them had a pad and pencil in his hands, scribbling down the license-plate number on the battered truck that was pulling away from the curb.

"Don't slow down!" Rand exclaimed. "Whatever they are, they're looking at us kind of suspiciously too."

As they pulled past the blue sedan Nicole realized he was right. "They're looking at everybody suspiciously, like bodyguards or something." She gasped and turned her eyes back to the road, her hand covering her mouth. "Oh, Rand! You don't suppose . . ."

"Hold that thought," he said, his expression grim, "and step on the gas, Nicole. For better or worse, good guys or bad, I do believe the government has arrived."

CHAPTER NINE

Nicole tried everything she could think of to lose the blue sedan. She twisted and turned, sped up and slowed down, even managed to get lost herself for a moment or two. Nothing worked. The three men who had captured Koslyn kept coming.

"I think we've had it, Rand," she admitted at last.

"We're outmatched." Nicole's imported car was a four-cylinder, front-wheel-drive model, economical and nimble but hardly capable of outrunning the powerful American car on their tail. "And they're getting impatient," he added, glancing over his shoulder. "They'll quit fooling around and do something desperate soon."

"Darn it," Nicole muttered nervously. "Where are we, Rand? I'm lost again."

"Take another left up there."

Nicole gnawed on her lower lip. "We've got to stop this. Somebody's going to get hurt. In the movies they clear all the noncombatants off the streets before filming a car chase."

"I said left, not right!" Rand cried. "This'll put us on the freeway!" The blue car squealed around the right-hand corner only moments behind them. "Too late. They've got us now. Our only hope was to outmaneuver them."

"Don't yell at me! I'm not Steve McQueen, you know."

"Sorry. I couldn't have done any better," Rand told her, his hand resting reassuringly on her thigh. "They would've had us, anyway. The guy behind the wheel obviously is trained for this sort of thing."

They zipped down the on ramp and into the light flow of traffic. Though she pressed the accelerator to the floor, the big sedan pulled alongside them easily.

"Why is Koslyn grinning like that?" she asked.

"Because misery loves company. He knows we'll be joining him in that backseat soon."

"Shall we give up?"

Rand sighed heavily. "I don't see how we have any choice in the matter. Who knows? Maybe they're the good guys," he said, though he didn't believe it for a second.

The man in the passenger seat was motioning for them to pull over. Nicole nodded and started to slow down. But Rand pushed on her knee, forcing her foot down on the gas. She glanced at him and saw that he was frowning.

"If you have an idea, I wish you'd let me in on it," she told him irritably.

"Maybe. Roll down your window." She did so,

and Rand motioned for the man in the passenger seat of the other car to do the same. "Who are you?" he yelled.

"Federal agents," the man yelled back. "Pull over."

Rand thought for a moment. "If you're who you say you are, you'll follow us to the nearest police station. We will surrender ourselves there."

The man's answer was quick and harsh. "No! Pull that car over right now, or we'll force you off the road!"

"They don't want us to turn ourselves in to the police, Nicole," Rand said thoughtfully. "Do they sound like fine, upstanding emissaries of our government to you?"

"No," she replied. "Not that it makes any difference." She tightened her grip on the steering wheel. "Because here they come."

The blue sedan edged into Nicole's lane. She drifted over as far as she could, the gritty debris on the shoulder of the road grinding beneath her tires. The small car bounced alarmingly on the rough surface.

"I'm going to have to slow down, Rand."

He nodded. "Give it up. We've done our best."

Then the radio squawked. *Vive la France!*"

"Vin!"

"Move it or lose it!"

A battered old pickup truck was directly behind the blue sedan. Ancient though it was, however, it still had plenty of life in it, much like the elderly madman at the wheel. Unencumbered by smog devices and built in the era of heavy steel, the truck had more than enough strength to take on the car in front of it. With a roar it surged forward and smacked the tormentors soundly in the rear end.

Rand and Nicole heard the collective exclamation of the four men in the other car. Koslyn seemed to be yelling the loudest, which was understandable, considering that he was handcuffed and couldn't hold on to anything like the other three. Vin hit them again. The driver had no alternative but to abandon the attack on Nicole's car and concentrate on controlling his own vehicle.

He sped up. Vin bounced him again. The truck was now beside Rand and Nicole. Vin waved merrily at them, his maniacal grin either frightening or reassuring, depending upon which side of his truck's bumper one was on.

"Orchid, you're crazy!" Nicole cried gleefully. "I love you!"

"See you later, Red Rose. I think I shall kick them all the way to Boulder." Vin waved again. "Take care of her, Toadstool."

"Give me that mike," Rand demanded, taking the radio microphone away from her. "You get away from them as soon as you can, Orchid. Do you hear me?"

"Yes, Toadstool," came the crackling reply.

"And stop calling me Toadstool!"

"Vive la liberté!"

The driver of the blue sedan was accelerating

away. Vin roared ahead, caught them, and put another sizable dent in their trunk. Nicole got off the shoulder of the road and took the next exit ramp.

It took her a moment to get her bearings, then she realized they weren't far from her apartment. Wary of every car that passed them now, Nicole made her way there on back streets, only to find that such caution was a waste of time.

"Did you leave the kitchen light on?" she asked Rand.

"You mean, you didn't?"

Parking the car in a back alley among the trash bins, the pair crept up to Nicole's back door and peeked through the window. Perhaps Jean had gotten worried and had come to wait for them there.

If it was Jean, she had taken up some radical form of interior decorating. Everything that could be pried loose or dumped out was on the kitchen floor. And from the sounds coming from the living room, the redecorating was still in progress.

"My things!" Nicole exclaimed, reaching for the door knob. "I'll murder those idiots!"

Rand took her by the arm and pulled her back toward the car. "It might turn out the other way around, dear. Come on. Let's get out of here."

This time Rand took the wheel. Nicole had had enough automotive thrills for one night. Though it seemed a year ago now, they remembered the hotel room they had paid for just that afternoon, a room that was waiting for them across town. Throwing caution to the wind, Rand jumped on the freeway and exceeded the speed limit all the way there.

But once again, they were too late. Parked in the lot near the entrance to the hotel was a blue sedan, its rear bumper and trunk battle-scarred from its encounter with Vin.

"How many of these guys *are* there?" Rand wondered aloud.

"Enough," Nicole grumbled dejectedly. "What I'd like to know is if they're working together or separately. If only Koslyn hadn't gotten caught!"

Feeling as though the whole world were watching him, Rand pulled through the parking lot and back out onto the street, constantly glancing in the rearview mirror.

"This is crazy! I'm beginning to get the feeling that they know our every move no matter how hard we try to be sneaky," he said, his face haggard and starting to reveal how tired he felt. "Together or not, one group or the other must have been tailing us all the time, and we didn't even know it."

"We're amateurs, Rand," she said soothingly, moving closer to him and placing her hand on his shoulder. "Even considering all our mistakes, I think we've done pretty well so far. We're still free, we've still got the real tape, and we're still together."

He took her hand and kissed her palm. "Thanks, I needed that," he murmured softly.

"You seem to be thinking a bit more clearly than I am at the moment. What do you suggest we do now?"

"In a way I think we've already done something pretty smart without even knowing it," she replied, deep in thought.

Rand chuckled. "Do tell. It would be nice to know we're not totally incompetent."

"Whoever they are, good guys or bad, in cahoots or not, we must have them spread pretty thin by now, don't you think?" Nicole asked. "I mean, they're probably watching your place, and we know there's somebody at my place and at the hotel back there. The one group has Koslyn, so he's out of the way, and the fake tape should be keeping someone busy."

"Not for long, though. I'll bet they're quite capable of figuring out that it's bogus."

She shrugged. "Even so, it should give us some time. Like you said, how many of them can there be?"

"Time for what?" Rand asked.

"To get some rest, for one thing," Nicole answered, stifling a yawn. "I'm as tired as you look. Once they figure out we tricked Koslyn, they'll stop vandalizing our property and start trying to vandalize us." It amazed her how she could make such a statement so calmly. Perhaps Rand was right. Maybe the human mind and body did develop a tolerance to danger. "While they're licking their wounds and planning their assault we need to find a safe house and do some regrouping of our own."

"Oh, yes. Go to ground, as they say in the pulps," he said, nodding in agreement. "Any ideas as to where?"

"No hotels. I'm developing a distinct preference for places with more than one exit."

"Me too." He thought for a moment. "My family's out. None of them live in Colorado. And your family is out because they *do* live here and therefore could be under surveillance already."

"Friends?" Nicole suggested.

Rand pulled into the drive-through of a fast-food restaurant and bought them some coffee. They sat in the car, engine running just in case, and sipped at the hot, rejuvenating liquid.

"Friends," Rand muttered. "Heck of a way to treat a friend, isn't it? Getting them involved in this mess?"

Nicole laughed, starting to feel human again. She would dearly love a shower and a soft bed. The thought of sleeping next to Rand again made her feel warm inside, a feeling she knew she should be wary of but simply couldn't ignore any longer.

"Maybe a rich friend," she said lazily, finding herself cuddling up to him. "You know, one who has a house he or she isn't using."

"Bingo!" Rand put the car in gear and pulled out of the parking lot so fast, Nicole almost spilled her coffee all over him. "It just so happens I have a friend like that. He's a little bit strange," he told her, waggling his hand to indicate some-one with a few loose marbles, "but he does have a place we can use as a base. I could kick myself for not thinking of it sooner."

"We didn't really need it until now." Visions of plush carpeting and a sunken tub danced before her eyes. "Where is this place? Is it nice?"

"Nice?" Rand frowned. "I guess you could call it that. Anyway, it's perfect. Close in, yet away from it all."

Away from it all? The plush carpeting vanished from her pleasant vision. "I don't like the sound of this."

"You'd rather sleep in the car?"

Nicole sighed. "As long as there's plenty of hot water, I'll be happy."

"All the comforts of home," he assured her.

They found a telephone booth, and Rand called his friend while Nicole watched from the car. They talked for quite a long time, consider-ing it was after midnight.

"You must know him well," she observed when he returned to the car and pulled back on the road. "I would have thought a conversation at this hour would be pretty one-sided."

"I've known Jim since college. He was an En-glish major, used to proofread my term papers for me," Rand explained. "He was just, um, telling me one of his tall tales."

"Tales?" she asked.

"He's a writer."

Nicole gazed at him curiously, wondering what

had made him so nervous all of a sudden. "What does he write?"

"Fiction. Boy, talk about a vivid imagination!"

"What kind of fiction?"

"Oh, far-out stuff."

"Such as?"

Rand chuckled uneasily. "Horror stories," he replied, then promptly changed the subject. "He said we're welcome to use the cabin as long as we can . . . I mean, as long as we want. We'll have to pick up some supplies, though. I gather he left the place in a bit of a hurry the last time he was up there and hasn't been back in a week or so."

"Why am I getting the feeling I'd rather sleep in the car?" She stared at him suspiciously. "Just what kind of tale did he tell you, Rand?"

He chuckled again. "You have to know Jim. He's always trying out new ideas on people, to see if he can scare them. I never take him too seriously."

"Something happened at this cabin of his, is that it?"

"Don't be silly. As I said, he was just telling me another of his tall tales." Rand rolled down his window, inhaling the warm night air. He glanced at the sky. "At least we won't have any trouble finding the place in the dark. Just look at that full moon!"

"This place doesn't look like it even has indoor plumbing, let alone hot water," Nicole said when they finally reached the cabin.

Rand turned off the engine but left the lights on so they could see to get their things to the rough-hewn front porch. He laughed, then leaned over and gave her a reassuring hug.

"Everything up here looks ramshackle on the outside. That way, no passing stranger will think there's anything worth stealing on the inside," he explained. "It's much nicer than it looks. Honest."

It wasn't the Taj Mahal by a long shot, but it was clean, cozy, and, as Rand had promised, was equipped with all the comforts of home. Before she would let him bring in her suitcase, however, she checked the bathroom.

"Hot water," she said with a relieved sigh as she rejoined him in the room that comprised the cabin's living room, dining room, and kitchen. "And a nice, deep tub."

"A feather bed too." Rand patted the fluffy mattress, his eyes gleaming with anticipation. "For after your bath."

Nicole knew exactly what he had in mind. Now that they were safe, all their trials and tribulations temporarily at bay, she was more than ready for a little comforting herself. If the anticipation of danger could be stimulating, living through that danger was even more of an aphrodisiac.

She wasn't about to give in without teasing him a bit, however. *"Our* bath," Nicole corrected. "You're just as dusty from that roof as I am."

"If you insist." He laughed wickedly, advancing toward her. "But we made a date on that roof for later, remember? And later has arrived."

Rand was stalking her around the living room, rubbing his hands together in anticipation. The muted overhead light cast giant shadows along the walls, mimicking his motions. He looked like some crazed character out of one of his friend's horror novels, except that she wasn't the least bit frightened of his sensual attack. In fact, she was laughing.

"I had a completely different seduction scene in mind," she informed him.

"Oh, really?" That stopped him. "What?"

Her voice was soft and husky, enticing him into her web. "A little cognac to help us relax, nice soothing warm water to wash away our troubles, and then . . ."

"Go on," he urged, his heart pounding like a gong at the sensuous picture she was painting.

Nicole smiled, teasing him with her eyes. "And then . . ."

"Then what? You can't stop now!"

"Mmm," she hummed, running the tip of her tongue over her lips, deliberately baiting him. "I'd thought we'd work on that part together, in the bath. See what we can come up with."

"I've already come up with something," he murmured.

"So I see," she returned saucily, slipping the zipper of her pantsuit down a few inches more to reveal the pearly-white skin in the valley between her breasts. "I think you'd better hurry with our suitcases, don't you?"

Rand stumbled down the stairs in his haste to get back to her. With economical movements he grabbed everything out of the car and locked it up for the night.

"Damnation," he said with a groan, hurrying back into the cabin and dropping everything in the bedroom. "The lights."

Once again he strode outside, unlocked the car, and turned off the headlights. Night closed in around him, dark and eerie, the full moon casting weird shadows as it peeked through the trees. Rand wished he hadn't listened to Jim's tall tale of the horrendous beast that stalked these woods. Then he heard a crackling noise coming from the underbrush. With undue haste he returned to the cabin and locked the door.

The sound of gushing water drew him toward the bathroom, all thoughts of things that go bump in the night forgotten. In his mind's eye he now saw only Nicole, her long legs and pert, succulent breasts waiting for him, teasing him.

"Did you find any brandy?" Nicole called out before he reached the bathroom door.

Rand reversed his direction and went to the kitchen. On his third try he found the liquor supply he knew Jim always kept well stocked. "Do you have a preference?"

"Surprise me," Nicole answered as she sank into the warm water. "Mmm. As long as it's expensive. I'm starting to feel like a million bucks."

Whatever she was doing in that tub, it was giving her voice a dreamy quality, and he intended to join that dream without further delay. Grabbing a bottle and glasses, he hurried to the bathroom. The sight of her made his breath catch in his throat.

"Join me?" she whispered, stretching her arms over her head, one hand held out in invitation as she relaxed in the big tub.

Rand drank in the sight of her. Her naked body was as enticing as her alluring smile. Her blond hair was pinned up, a few strands escaping the topknot. "Try stopping me."

"The water's ready," she murmured, skimming her hands along the calm surface and letting the rivulets run down the creamy length of her arms.

"So am I." With each breath she took, the rosy tips of her breasts peeked out at him, then slipped back beneath the transparent covering of water. "Here I come."

"It's better without your clothes," she encouraged, taking the half full snifter he offered.

Rand filled his glass and set it down on the redwood edging. One smooth white leg rose gracefully out of the water, toes pointed, foot arched. With her toes she beckoned him. His fingers seemed to be all thumbs as he hastily stripped off his clothes.

"Are these water jets?" Nicole asked, covering a chrome circle with her hand.

He nodded his head in agreement and pulled open a small door hidden by the wood design. A few flicks of his wrist and water was churning around her.

Rand wasn't the only one admiring the sights. As he leaned over the controls the motion accentuated the firm lines of his thighs, his leg muscles outlined in curves and masculine indentations, flowing into lean buttocks and hips. His back rippled with each movement, making her want to know every line intimately.

"All right?"

"Mmm," she murmured, half closing her eyes and sipping her drink, her gaze never leaving him. "Perfect."

The tip of her tongue flicked out to catch a precious drop of cognac and pull it into her mouth. Rand wanted Nicole to take him inside her the same way. Carefully he slid into the bubbling water and eased down beside her.

She held her glass to his lips, wanting him to drink from the same spot, the thought of his mouth covering hers undeniably sensuous. As he sipped the heady liquor he felt the rushing fire of its potency burn through him, an added fuel to their desire.

Rand cradled her face between his hands, stroking the curves of her jaw as his mouth found hers. White heat enveloped him, her tongue intertwining with his, the fevered, intimate touch communicating their mutual need. Nicole felt as if her blood were carbonated, like the bubbling water surrounding them.

Her fingers were caressing his chest, the

pounding of his heart vibrating against her hand. Slender fingers curled around the short hairs before skimming the edges of his ribs and downward. The palm of her hand slid back and forth across the planes of his stomach, inching lower and lower.

Then she stopped abruptly. "What was that?" Nicole whispered, jumping nervously.

Rand jumped too. Her nails were digging into his sides, and the pain jerked him into an upright position. "What? I didn't hear anything," he returned, carefully prying her gouging fingernails from him one by one.

Nicole listened intently, but the only noise she heard now was the gurgling water foaming around them. When Rand held his glass to her mouth, she drank from it, savoring the smooth, warming taste. Slowly she began to relax and leaned back against him, aware of his powerful masculinity.

"You see? It was nothing. Where were we?" he murmured, picking up her hand and placing it on his throbbing desire. "Yes. That's the spot."

Nicole feathered her lips along his throat and stroked the velvety smoothness of him, pleased by the raspy moaning sounds escaping from his chest. "Like that?" she asked, encircling him firmly with her teasing fingers.

"Definitely," he replied with a groan.

His arm slipped up her side, the coarse hairs a caress all their own. He cupped one silky white orb in his hand, teasing the pink tip into a hard bud with the lightly callused pad of his thumb. His lips blazed a path down her arching neck, his tongue dipping into the well of her ear.

"Definitely," she echoed, moaning. His caresses were sending liquid fire coursing through her veins, a nagging ache at the base of her thighs begging to be eased. "Yes!"

Sharp teeth were nibbling on the delicate skin of her earlobe, his tongue flitting across the base of her throat before his mouth captured the pebbled hardness of her breast.

Suddenly she jerked and pulled away from him. "There it was again!" she cried urgently. "I heard something!" Or someone, she thought, her eyes widening.

"Oh, Lord." Rand groaned, almost slipping beneath the water. He was about to explode with a need he could barely control and she was hearing things. "It's just the wind, Nicole."

"But the wind isn't blowing." She backed into the far corner of the tub. "Rand, I'm serious," she informed him anxiously.

He closed his eyes and rested his head against the edge of the tub, listening. Was there something out there? No, it was just his imagination. Actually it was Jim's imagination. The next time Rand spoke with him he'd tell him to keep his beastly tales of giant wolves to himself.

"Do—"

"Ssh! I'm listening," he ordered, cocking his head toward the open door. Nothing. "I don't hear a thing, Nicole." Then something definitely went bump in the night. The hair on the back of his neck stood at attention. "Oh. That's just a squirrel."

"Go see!" she insisted fiercely, her arms crossed over her breasts.

Rand sighed loudly and heaved himself out of the water. He knew that the only way his aching desire was going to be assuaged was to convince her there was nothing nasty creeping around outside. Creatures, ghosts, and ghoulies indeed! It was just a squirrel. Maybe.

"Where are you going?"

"You told me to go see, remember?"

"And leave me here alone?" She gasped.

He pulled a thick towel around his middle and stepped into his shoes. "If I stay with you, will you forget this nonsense?"

She thought about it for a moment. "Be careful."

"Right. You have to watch those man-eating squirrels," he muttered under his breath as he left her in the bathroom.

Wonderful. If there was something out there, he didn't have a gun or any other means of solid defense. His fist didn't count. He could just imagine taking a swing with one hand while holding his towel up with the other. Wrapping the towel tightly around his middle, he twisted it snugly to his body, freeing his hands.

Then he heard the noise again. All right, so it was a great big squirrel. The mountain air must agree with them. At least it wasn't a sneaky noise, like one of the spies creeping up on them. A secret agent wouldn't bang around like this thing was doing. Thing?

Rand took an abrupt detour into the kitchen. Pulling open drawer after drawer, he at last found what he wanted, a huge, shiny butcher knife, its sharp point gleaming in the dim, eerie light. He chuckled nervously.

"Silly," he said to himself. With studied nonchalance he lit the oil lamp on the mantel of the stone fireplace. "The better to see you with, my dear. Now, if I was to hear a howling in the night—"

Something scratched just outside the front door. Then it grunted, snorted, and sniffed. The match Rand had used to light the lamp burned down to his fingertips.

"Ouch!"

"Are you all right?" Nicole asked in a quavering voice.

"Just peachy," Rand grumbled. "Stay there."

Stealthily he crept over to the door, unlocking and flinging it wide open. Only the stillness of the night leapt out to greet him. With cautious steps he checked the front porch and the sides of the house.

Nicole was right. The night air was calm, without a breath of wind. An almost eerie quiet engulfed him. He stepped around the back of the cabin, stopping in his tracks when a loud crackling sound pierced the silence. His pulse soared ahead erratically, the ceramic oil lamp shaking in his hand as he stared out into the dense blackness of the forest. He gripped the handle of the knife firmly and held it at ready.

Something was out there, all right. Quite close. Rand crouched, catlike, making his way into the trees, the glow of the oil lamp flickering wildly with each step he took. The crackling noise grew louder, then suddenly seemed to come from directly over his head. He jerked the lamp up so fast, the flame guttered and died, but not before he saw the gleaming yellow eyes of the beast as it dropped on him.

Nicole jumped and splashed water all over the bathroom floor when she heard Rand cry out. When she could no longer stand the silence that followed, she rose slowly out of the tub and wrapped a towel around her trembling form. Heart pounding, she crept silently over to the bathroom door, peered around the corner, and looked out the open front door to where the light spilling from the living room ended and pitch-black vagueness began. She couldn't see anything in the darkness beyond.

But there was a huge shadow moving across the porch. Just as Nicole was trying to decide whether to yell a warning to Rand or keep quiet, a huge, gleaming knife appeared in the doorway. She promptly let out a bloodcurdling scream.

Rand practically flew into the cabin, intent on protecting her at any cost. "Did you see something?"

"You did that on purpose!" she accused.

"What? Why did you scream? Is someone here?" he asked, his words coming in a rush as he looked around him.

She backed up toward the bedroom, her anger apparent as she pointed a finger at the offending object. "You—you held that knife in front of the door."

"Is that all?" His shoulders slumped. "You scared me half to death!"

"I s-scared *y-you?*" she spluttered in outrage. "That stunt just bought you a night on the floor, Rand!"

Rand had had enough. Not only had Nicole's nervousness interrupted his pleasures but also his own wild imagination had practically given him a heart attack. Now she was accusing him of frightening her on purpose and had banished him from her bed. And for what? All he'd found outside was a whole family of raccoons playing merrily in the trees, not disturbed by his company in the least.

He dropped the butcher knife on a table, set the lamp down, slammed the door shut, and locked it securely. His towel slid to the floor as he advanced in her direction, his shoes left by the wayside.

"Are you afraid of cute, fuzzy little animals?"

"Of course not. Is that—"

"Have you heard any other strange noises?"

"Just you yelling. But—"

"Did you see anyone?"

"N-no." She took another step back. The look in his hazel eyes was menacing. Had he gone mad out there in the dark? "Rand, what are you going to do?"

"Guess!" With a quick jerk her towel floated freely to the floor. He flipped her up over his shoulder and strode into the bedroom.

Nicole pounded on his back in outrage. "What are you doing? I'm mad at you. You're sleeping on the floor!"

"You and I," he announced, dropping her on the bed, "have some unfinished business to attend to." His body covered hers before she could even begin to move.

"Rand! How dare you use these caveman tactics on me?"

"Like this, love," he murmured, fitting his body snugly against her squirming form, enjoying her every move. "Any other silly questions?"

Nicole worked her arm free of his body and grabbed hold of his hair. "Listen to me!"

"You're not saying anything I want to hear. But your body is. It's speaking my language." With ease he removed her hand and pinned it securely to the bed above her head. "It knows what it wants. And so does mine."

She could feel the heat of his masculinity pressing against her thigh, teasing her with his warmth. She wanted him but not in this dominating way. She fought the strong response of her body to his, her mind in turmoil.

Rand could feel the struggle seesawing through

183

her. To give in to his dominance wasn't her way. He smiled at her. He would make it easy for her this time. At the moment he needed her too much to fight that particular battle, and he wanted her completely, without reservation.

Nicole felt his weight shifting off her and didn't know whether to be happy or disappointed. Rand didn't give her time to worry. He slipped to her side, his legs still holding hers firmly in place. With startling quickness he took her other hand and held it, too, above her head. His free hand caressed her cheek fleetingly before feathering across her breasts and down the front of her body. He cupped her femininity intimately.

Her voice came out in a breathy gasp. "Rand!"

"Yes, love?" he said soothingly, using his legs to hold hers still, spreading them apart. His fingers were caressing her softly, teasingly, not giving her what she wanted and needed. "Do you want me?"

"Yes! Yes!" she cried, his touch taunting but not satisfying her. "Now."

"What's the hurry?" he crooned, slipping between her legs. Her hips rose up to greet him, guiding him, seeking him feverishly.

They fused together in an explosion of desire, leaping higher and higher on a cresting wave, riding out the raging fire storm within them. Fast and furious, the crash came upon them, sending them hurtling into a swirling maelstrom of blissful release.

Rand rolled over, pulling her still quivering

form on top of him, his hands willingly soothing the damp skin beneath his touch.

"Rand," she said softly.

"Ssh, love, sleep," he whispered, cradling her to him.

"Was there anything out there?"

"A family of raccoons." He laughed quietly. He had stalked the poor creatures like criminals, and they'd completely ignored him. Some threat he was! "I almost jumped out of my skin when one of them fell out of a tree at my feet."

"Oh, I'd like to see them. Are they still out there?" she asked, raising her head sleepily.

"No, I chased them off," he said, lying blithely. There was no way he was going traipsing off with her into a forest in the middle of the night. "The mighty hunter saved you again."

"Mmm, too bad," she mumbled. She was soon fast asleep.

There was a thump and a bump, then the sound of something scratching at the bedroom window. Rand opened one eye and saw a baby raccoon staring at him.

"What are you trying to do," he whispered, "spoil my image?" Almost as if it understood, the creature scampered off, and Rand joined the woman he loved in dreamland.

CHAPTER TEN

"Blood. I must have blood."

"Stop that! You're getting my neck all soggy, Rand," Nicole protested, laughing and pushing him away. She turned from the kitchen counter and handed him a cup. "Here, drink some coffee instead."

Rand took it gratefully. "Smells wonderful. Thanks." He sat down at the butcher-block table near the cabin's dominant picture window, looking out at the forest around them. Nicole joined him. "Wild night," he said, arching his eyebrows roguishly. "In more ways than one."

"Let's just say not all of the beasts were outside," she agreed, gazing at him mischievously. "If I ever get to meet this tale-telling friend of yours, I'm going to be torn between thanking him and having him committed."

"Well," Rand said, stretching lazily, "What should we two internationally famous detectives do today?"

Nicole was digging through her purse. "The

first thing we need to do is take stock of our funds. I've got three dollars, how about you?"

"Five," he said after looking in his wallet. "Sleuthing takes its toll on the pocketbook."

"The car needs gas, and we'll need running-around—or is that running-away?—money. I have a gas company credit card, so that's no problem, but I didn't think to bring my checkbook with me."

"Neither did I. But," he added, pulling a card out of his wallet, "all we have to do is find one of those automatic teller machines and we're in business."

"Oh." Nicole fished her access card out of her purse. "I have one of those too. I guess we're not completely cut off from the world, are we?"

Rand got up and stood behind her, leaning over to give her a hug. "Feeling put upon today, my love?"

Her heart skipped a beat at his casual endearment. But she knew he didn't mean it in a serious way. They were just two people who had been thrown together, with no one to turn to for comfort and sympathy but each other. Their tempestuous attraction was a rose among the thorny danger surrounding them, and she dared not think too much about what tomorrow would bring.

"I'm just anxious for things to return to normal, that's all," Nicole replied. "I want to walk through my greenhouses. I want to be there for the big family dinner they'll have when my mother and father get back from their vacation. And I'd much rather be planning a new sales strategy than figuring ways to outwit a bunch of spies."

Rand stiffened slightly. She hadn't mentioned how he fit into her plans. "How normal do you think either of us will be after all this?" he asked.

"You know what I mean. Business as usual, a quiet life with no one tearing up my apartment. Maybe you and I can even get back to our familiar rivalry," she added in a teasing tone.

"I see." He returned to his seat, a perturbed frown furrowing his brow. "I guess I was being overly optimistic. A Sabine never forgets," he muttered.

"Excuse me?"

"Nothing." He sipped at his coffee, hiding a smile of bitter determination. Nicole would be his, completely and forever, or he would rather not come out of this mess at all. "Once we get gas in the car and money in our pockets, what then?" Rand asked. "Read any good books lately?"

"Hmm," she said thoughtfully. "When those guys picked up Koslyn, we lost our advantage. Now they know we have the tape, simply because we knew enough about it to make a fake one."

"I hadn't thought about it like that."

"So," Nicole continued, "they're going to be even more anxious to speak with us than they were before. That may give us an advantage of a sort."

Rand looked at her, obviously skeptical. "Such as?"

"Before last night, I think they were just watching us, keeping tabs on us, so to speak. But they sure moved in quick when they thought we'd made a deal with Koslyn."

"Didn't they, though," Rand commented sourly. "I wonder if they tore up my house the way they tore up your apartment."

Nicole's face reddened with anger. "Don't remind me. After this is all over I hope there's somebody we can hold accountable for all the damage." She fumed silently for a moment. "Where was I? Oh, yes. They moved fast last night. They'll move even faster now, and they might even get careless. What if we turn the tables on them, like we did with Koslyn, only a bit more daring?"

"More daring than setting up a rogue cop? I like the sound of it already," Rand replied, grinning. Every time they did something like this, they ended up in each other's arms. And every moment together was a golden opportunity to make her feel the same emotions he felt building within himself. "Go on."

"We can't meet with them. They know we've got the tape, and they don't strike me as the bargaining type. Besides, I imagine they're too sharp to fall for the kind of trick we pulled on Koslyn, anyway." She smiled broadly, too, warming to her own idea. "But since we know where they'll be, couldn't we sneak up on them from behind?"

"I saw that movie!" Rand exclaimed, catching her excitement. "This guy is being watched, so he makes it look like he's still in his house, sneaks out, then follows the bad guys back to their lair when they change shifts."

"Right! Of course, they don't know where we are right now, so they're not watching us, but they're watching our homes. With as many blunders as we've made, I'm sure they think we'll stumble into their net soon."

Rand's smile disappeared. "Wait a minute. I think that guy got caught in that movie, didn't he?"

"Well, yes," she admitted. "But he wanted to confront the bad guys. All we want to do is see who they are."

"That's right. Somebody around here has to be honest," Rand reasoned. "What we need to do is follow everybody we can, determine which of them seem to be up to no good, and give the tape to whoever is left."

"Simple."

Rand laughed. "The direct approach, at any rate. We'd better get moving."

They grabbed their surveillance gear and got ready to leave. In the car, bouncing down the rutted drive leading away from the cabin, the enormity of their task seemed to hit them both at the same time.

"Has it occurred to you," Rand asked, "that we may be just the tiniest bit crazy?"

Nicole nodded grimly. "It just did. What on

earth do we think we're doing? The people who are after us are trained professionals."

"Still, I don't see any alternative. They wouldn't let us give up now even if we wanted to. We know too much."

"Depressingly true," Nicole agreed. "Being a concerned, patriotic citizen does have its downside. You have to take on the responsibility of doing the right thing." She closed her eyes for a moment and tried to think calmly. "I guess we have to look at our successes. We did fool Koslyn, right?"

"Yes. But he was greedy."

"So are the other guys, though. We can't be sure the men in the blue car are after the tape for profit, but it's a pretty good bet. They weren't willing to allow us to turn ourselves in to the police."

Rand pulled onto the main road and headed for Denver, thankful to be on a smooth surface again. It looked as if it was going to be a glorious day, at least as far as the weather was concerned. The early-morning sun was shining in a clear blue sky, making it difficult to stay worried about anything for long.

"They may just want the glory of rounding up the tape and us all to themselves, I suppose," Rand said, thinking aloud. "But I'm suspicious of anyone who calls himself a Federal agent yet infringes on the rights he's supposedly sworn to protect."

"They're all so heavy-handed," Nicole complained. "I know that there has to be somebody out there who has the country's best interests at heart, but really! Breaking and entering, vandalizing private property. I doubt the people searching my apartment last night had a warrant." She looked at Rand, perturbed and confused. "How are we going to tell the good guys from the bad guys, even if we do manage to follow them without getting caught?"

"Good question." He drove on in silence for a while, thinking. "Personally I am inclined to believe we haven't seen any good guys yet and that we'll know them when we do."

"How?" she asked sardonically. "Their white hats?"

Rand shot her a sidelong glance. "No, dear. But I think they'll show other signs of goodness, such as an open, honest approach and a pronounced concern with doing things by the book."

"I thought you were cynical of the so-called intelligence community?"

"I am. Most post-Watergate Americans are. But that's precisely my point. Dirty tricks don't sit well with people these days," he explained, "no matter how noble the cause. It has been generally agreed upon in this country that the ends do not necessarily justify the means. We have laws, and except in the most unusual of circumstances even secret agents are obliged to follow them."

Nicole sniffed disdainfully. "You, my dear, are an incurable optimist."

"That's me," Rand agreed amiably, putting his arm around her shoulder. "I am full of faith that the future will be bright." His hand wandered down to gently caress the side of her breast. "And the present isn't so bad, either."

"Rand! Concentrate on the road!"

"My mind is on other curves," he murmured huskily.

She took his hand and put it back on the wheel. "Then pull over and let me drive."

"How about I pull over and we hop in the backseat?"

"You're incorrigible."

Why did she have so little control of her own body when Rand was near? Spots of color had appeared on her cheeks, and the sensitive tips of her breasts were sending urgent messages to her very core.

She didn't know which had her more worried, the situation they were in or the definite possibility that she was falling head over heels in love with him. Would she still feel the same way when this was over? Or was it just a side effect of the excitement?

Time would tell, but that was a problem too. For the foreseeable future she and Rand were destined to spend their days and nights together, days of being forced to trust each other and nights spent in each other's arms. Hardly the ideal circumstance for making rational decisions. In fact, it was a good way to lose her heart to a man who might easily break it in two.

Luckily, they were nearing a shopping center, giving her a good reason to interrupt both his playful touch and the very serious thoughts that touch provoked within her.

"Look. There's an automatic teller machine in the parking lot up ahead," she told him.

"As long as we're stopping, let's get some gas too." He pointed at the station on the opposite corner. "That place has good prices."

They filled the car, then parked and went to the automatic teller. Rand used his card to open the door, and they stepped into the glass kiosk, grateful that it was air-conditioned. Rand put his card into the waiting slot and punched in his secret code. The machine promptly spit his card back out.

"Darn thing!" He tried it again, with the same result.

"What's wrong? Don't you have any money in your account?" Nicole asked.

Rand glared at her. "Of course I do. Maybe the machine is low on cash, or . . ." He trailed off, his eyes widening in alarm. "Government agents," he said in an ominous tone. "You don't suppose they've seized our bank accounts?"

"Don't be silly!" Nicole replied nervously. "Why would they do that?"

"To keep us from getting enough money to get away."

It made a certain kind of terrifying sense. Nicole elbowed him aside. "That's crazy. Here, let me try my card." She put it into the slot and entered her code, fingers trembling. The machine clicked and whirred, then gave her her card back. "It won't take mine, either," she said with a groan. "Oh, Lord, Rand. What if they've cut us off completely? What if they do the same to my family? We'll be ruined. Our creditors—"

"Calm down!" he demanded. "The gas station took your credit card, didn't they?"

"Oh." She breathed a sigh of relief. "You're right."

"Here. I'll try mine again," Rand announced.

Nicole grabbed his hand before he could put his card into the slot. "No! It won't give your card back this time. You only get three chances to get your number right, in case it's someone who stole your card but doesn't know the code."

"Are you saying I don't know my own number?"

Digging through her purse, Nicole found a piece of paper with her access number on it. This time she carefully entered the code, making sure she got it right. The machine almost cheerfully gave her some money.

She sagged against the wall and closed her eyes. "Whew! For a minute there I thought Big Brother really was watching us. I had this vision of the floor opening up and swallowing us both."

"Now *that's* paranoid," Rand told her irritably. He looked in his wallet, found his own hidden reminder of his correct code number, and tried the machine a third time. "Still, one can't be too careful." As the computer whirred, he kept a cautious eye on the floor beneath his feet.

Nicole burst out laughing when it fulfilled his request for cash. "Are we a pair? How are we going to trail trained spies when we can't even withdraw money properly?"

"That's our real advantage," Rand informed her, chuckling with her as they returned to the car. "They'll never expect us to do something so dumb. As a matter of fact, even if they do catch us, they'll probably be laughing so hard, we'll get away again."

The people watching Rand's house weren't laughing. In fact, it was hard to imagine less jovial individuals. From their vantage point, hidden among the shade trees of a nearby park, Rand and Nicole had yet to see one of the men as much as smile.

Surprisingly, for such a beautiful afternoon, the park wasn't busy, only a handful of children and a few adults enjoying the green grass and spreading elms. On the other side of the dense foliage where they stood, a fountain bubbled happily. Beside it, a young woman with curly black hair sat on a bench reading a book and gently bouncing a stroller with her foot.

Thanks to the amazing directional microphone, the pair were able to stay a safe distance away and yet still hear and record everything that happened on the other side of the park. Safe distance or not, however, they had taken the precaution of changing their appearance. Nicole felt rather mysterious and sexy in her dark glasses and makeshift disguise.

"I hope people who do this kind of thing for a living get paid well for it," Rand remarked, lowering the binoculars from his eyes, "because it's the most boring job on earth."

Nicole nodded. "It could be worse, though." She was sitting on a blanket they had spread on the ground, nibbling on the remains of their picnic lunch, her back resting against a gnarled old oak tree. "At least we're out in the open air. Imagine how those two in the car feel."

There were four of them altogether. Two sat in a drab red station wagon across the street from Rand's house. The other pair, dressed in shorts and muscle shirts, were watching the house and playing a lackadaisical game of touch football on the edge of the park nearest the street. It was only apparent that they weren't what they pretended to be when they stopped a passersby and pointed at the house.

Nicole had them on tape: "Do you know Rand Jameson? Have you seen him lately? We're private investigators, ma'am, and we're trying to find him. His uncle just passed away and left him a great deal of money, but he'll lose it if he doesn't claim it soon."

They took turns asking the questions. Alternately Rand had either won the lottery, inherited a large sum of money, or was wanted for falling behind in his payments to his ex-wife. None of his neighbors seemed overly excited by the thought of Rand getting rich, unless there was a reward for finding him. It was surprising, though, how angry people he didn't know got about him not paying his alimony.

"I didn't know you'd been married," Nicole teased.

"Neither did I," Rand grumbled. "I'm going to have to move after this. Half the people in the neighborhood now think I'm a bum, while the other half are suddenly anxious to get to know a rich guy like me."

Nicole frowned. "What do you suppose they're telling my neighbors?" she wondered aloud.

"Here we go," Rand said excitedly. "The changing of the guard."

Nicole stood up and peered through the trees. The two men playing football were replaced by a pair who preferred baseball. The station wagon was replaced by a van with a landscaping advertisement on the side. The men who had been relieved met at the end of the block and drove off in the station wagon together.

Rand and Nicole weren't worried about losing their subjects. A one-way street wound around the park, and they had parked at the outlet. All they had to do was pack up, hurry to their car, and fall in behind the men when they finally threaded their way out of the park.

"Where did that girl with the stroller go?" Rand asked.

Nicole emerged from the trees right beside him. "Why?"

"She had nice legs," he returned, grinning.

"Beast!"

Rand ducked as she swung at him with their equipment bag, blocking the blow with the picnic basket. "What's wrong? Jealous?"

"Yes!" She was fuming, angry at herself for letting it show.

Obviously Rand had been right. The foursome in the station wagon didn't seem the slightest bit worried that someone might be following. Windows rolled up to enjoy the air-conditioning, they talked among themselves with never a backward glance. So far so good.

They made a stop at a convenience store, evidently for cigarettes, then at a liquor store for beer. A place that sold hero sandwiches was next on their list of off-duty priorities.

"This is it?" Nicole asked, disgusted. "We follow them around while they eat lunch?"

"At least we know they're not very concerned with the laws of the land. It's illegal to have a rolling beer party in this city."

"Hardly damning evidence they're bad guys, though."

Rand shrugged. "It's a start. I'm already convinced."

"You just say that because they impugned your name," she observed dryly. "Still, I suppose that wasn't very ethical, either. We don't have all the time in the world, Rand. Shall we drop this bunch and try the ones at my place?"

"Might as well." He sighed. "It looks like they're pulling into that adult motel up ahead. I don't expect angels, but I'm not turning the tape over to that group even if they *are* from our government."

Rand had great hopes for the next group. They weren't swilling beer or accosting strangers and telling lies about Nicole, nor were they pretending to be anything but what they were: a surveillance team. There were just two, a more reasonable number if they were civil servants on a budget-conscious government payroll. And most encouraging of all, they did smile occasionally.

"What do you think, Nicole?"

"Maybe," she replied, "if they get off work and go home to the wife and kids, we may have found the guys in the white hats. Of course," she added warily, "that still doesn't mean their superior's not dirty."

"Good point. But we'll never be certain."

"No. And we can't keep this up forever, either," she pointed out. "Sooner or later we'll have to choose the most likely candidates and set up a meeting."

Rand nodded. "I agree. Let's think about that for a while. It won't be easy to set things up so we can beat a hasty retreat in case the meeting takes a wrong turn."

Thinking was about all there was to do, anyway. There were no cool, green parks within spying distance of Nicole's apartment, making it necessary for them to use the parking lot of a nearby grocery store. They sat in the car, almost hidden from the street by a concrete retaining wall that ran along the front of the property. Luckily a cool breeze flowed through their open windows.

Their thoughts were interrupted, however, when a Sabine delivery van pulled up in front of the apartment complex across the street. The two men in the car straightened in their seats, suddenly alert. Jean got out of the van.

"What's she doing here?" Rand asked, watching Jean through his binoculars as she left the van and headed for Nicole's apartment.

"I don't know. Should we warn her?"

Rand frowned, focusing the binoculars on the two men. "They don't seem inclined to harass her. Wait a minute." He peered through the powerful lenses. "They have photographs of us, Nicole. They're comparing yours to Jean and shaking their heads. I'm liking these guys more all the time. Calm, collected, they seem to be real professionals."

"It's a shame there's too much noise around here to use the directional microphone. I'd give anything to hear what they're saying."

"Me too." He glanced at her. "I've got an idea. Jean just went into your apartment. Go to that pay phone in front of the grocery store, give her a call, and tell her to talk to those guys when she comes out."

Nicole's mouth dropped open. "Are you crazy?"

"Like a fox," he replied, grinning at her. "If any of these people were going to use your family as hostages, I think they'd have done it by now. And we're close by. Just tell her to ask them the time or something, get a good look at them, and report back to us over the radio in the van."

"Well, all right." She got out of the car. "I guess we do have to find out as much as we can about them. They're our best bet for good guys so far."

"But don't tell her where we are."

"Why not?"

He looked at her in surprise. "You mean it hasn't occurred to you that your phone is probably tapped?"

Her face pale, Nicole went to make the call. When she returned, she looked angrier than ever. At least the color was back in her cheeks. She slammed the car door hard and sat glaring across the street.

"I think you're right," she told him. "The phone sounded funny, scratchy or something. And from the way Jean described the damage, my apartment is in even worse shape than I thought it was last night. They wrecked the place!"

Rand patted her on the shoulder. "They'll get their just desserts. Did she say what she was doing there?"

"Watering the plants. She needn't have bothered. They'd already ripped them up."

"I'm sorry."

Calming herself, she turned and gave him a halfhearted smile. "I wonder how one goes about suing a spy?"

"If anyone can do it," he said, kissing her on the cheek, "Nicole Sabine will find a way. Did Jean agree to talk to the two men watching your place?"

Nicole grinned. "She's looking forward to it."

"Take pictures for the family album," Rand instructed, handing her the camera. He lifted the binoculars to his eyes. "Here she comes."

Jean walked out of the apartment, locked the door behind her, and strode across the lawn toward the two men. There was a flurry of activity in the car before she reached them, then they settled down and smiled at her when she arrived.

"I wish I could read lips," Nicole muttered.

"At least they're still smiling. That's a good sign."

"They're shaking their heads a lot too. I don't know whether that's a good sign or not."

Rand shrugged. "We'll know soon enough. She's going back to the van now. She's getting in." The radio beneath the dash of Nicole's car rasped with static. Rand grabbed the microphone. "Hello?"

"That's not how you do it," Nicole objected. She took the mike from him and spoke into it.

"Red Rose calling Pink Carnation. Come in, Pinky. Over."

"Pinky here. Hi, Red Rose," Jean replied. "And hello to you, too, Toadstool."

Rand groaned. "I am never going to live this down."

"What were they like, Pinky?" Nicole asked.

The radio crackled. "Real nice. Very polite and quite well mannered. Handsome devils too."

"Cut the dating report and ask her what they said," Rand demanded irritably.

Nicole chuckled. "What did they say, Pinky?"

"Beats me."

"What do you mean?"

"They didn't speak a word of English. I tried French, and one of them seemed to understand, but his accent was thick and my French isn't as good as yours, anyway."

Nicole and Rand looked at each other, equally depressed by the news. "Any idea what language they were speaking, Pinky?" she asked her sister.

"I don't know," Jean replied uncertainly. "You know I don't have an ear for languages. I don't even understand Grandpa half the time."

"Spanish-sounding or German-sounding?" Nicole pressed.

"Um, neither, really."

"Do you remember any words? This is important, Pinky. What sort of thing were they saying when they were shaking their heads?"

There was a pause. "Yet. That's what they

204

were saying," she replied. "They were shaking their heads and saying yet, yet."

"Thanks, Pinky. Go home now. And tell everyone we're bearing up just fine. Okay?"

"Okay. Take care. Over and out."

Nicole looked at Rand. He was slumped in his seat, his eyes closed. He blew out a deep breath in a forlorn sigh. "Yet. *Nyet.* Nicole, my sweet, we almost turned ourselves over to the Russians."

"What now, Comrade?" she asked, her tone full of gloom.

He rubbed his tired eyes, then straightened and looked at her dejectedly. "Find another bunch to watch, I guess. Maybe we'll go hang around your greenhouses for a while, see who shows up."

"You know," Nicole commented, "I find it rather odd that there are Russian agents on my doorstep and we're the only ones who seem at all interested in them."

"Maybe no one else knows they're here."

"A particularly naïve assumption on your part," a feminine voice informed him.

Rand whirled in his seat and found himself looking at a young woman with an olive complexion and curly black hair standing by his window. On the other side of the car there was a blond man similarly positioned next to Nicole's door. They had been so absorbed in discussing their next move that they hadn't noticed the pair approach them.

"You!" Rand exclaimed. "You're the woman from the park."

She smiled at him. "The one with the nice legs, I believe you said. Thanks for the compliment. I don't get them often in my line of work."

The nicely dressed, rather boyish-looking man bending down to Nicole's window hadn't said a word. She glared at him for a moment, then turned her attention to his genial feminine partner.

"And just what is your line of work?" Nicole demanded.

"Anything the president wants me to do," she replied pleasantly. "You can call me Marsha, and the strong, silent type over there is John. You see, we're the good guys you've been looking for."

"Oh, brother," Rand muttered. "John and Marsha. Not very creative, are you?"

The woman shrugged. "Look who's talking. I sort of like Red Rose, but Toadstool?"

"You've been eavesdropping on us?" Nicole asked, outraged. "And following us?"

Marsha nodded, smiling apologetically. "I'm afraid so."

"For how long?"

"Well, we got word of the fouled-up shipment rather late. Red tape." She laughed. "Red tape. What a horrible pun. Anyway, we did arrive in time to get some interesting aerial photographs of you scrambling around on a rooftop."

"What?" Nicole's face paled. "You were watching—"

"How do we know you're the good guys? Your actions don't sound very good to me," Rand interjected tersely. "We've been in some tight scrapes since then. If you're supposed to be the good guys, why didn't you pick us up before now?"

"Orders," Marsha replied. "You weren't in any real danger, and it was useful to us to allow you to roam around for a while. However," she added, her tone turning stern and chastising, "you did manage to lose us last night. We didn't pick you up again until this morning."

Rand tried not to show his relief at that revelation. He glanced at Nicole. She appeared just as wary as he was. "And that finally made you decide to save us?" he asked Marsha sarcastically.

"You're not very good at this, but you are getting better. And in this game a little knowledge can be a very dangerous thing. We're afraid you're going to get hurt."

"Besides," Nicole observed curtly, "you want to talk to us about the gap in your surveillance last night, right?"

Marsha sighed. "Among other things. You know very well what we want from you. Your country appreciates your help, but the time has come to unburden yourselves of this noble quest of yours. I should think you'd both be relieved."

Her partner spoke for the first time. "Step out of the car, please."

It was a request, not an order. John and Marsha were polite, efficient, and obviously good at their profession. Nicole and Rand looked at each other, confused. These were supposedly the people they had hoped to find. So why was it they didn't feel the slightest bit relieved?

"Are we under arrest?" Rand asked.

Nicole folded her arms over her breasts. "I want to call my lawyer," she informed them defiantly.

To their mutual surprise the woman calling herself Marsha chuckled heartily. "That's better. I was wondering when you two would stop playing secret agent and start acting like normal citizens again." She opened Rand's door. Her partner did the same for Nicole. "No, you're not under arrest. And yes, you may talk to a lawyer if you so desire."

Rand got out of the car, puzzled. The man called John offered Nicole his hand, and she climbed out as well. This was the way she had imagined it would be when they finally found the right people to turn the tape over to.

"But if we're not under arrest . . ."

"Why do you have to go with us?" Marsha completed. "You don't, Nicole. You, either, Rand. We would appreciate it if you would come with us and assist us in our investigation. It is possible for us to get either a warrant or a subpoena if you do not come willingly, but we'd rather not. Our car is this way."

"Wait a minute," Rand said. "I don't—"

"Please!" Marsha said, interrupting. She was getting impatient. And, like her partner at Nicole's side, she suddenly was nervous and alert also. "I know you have as many questions for us as we do for you. But I must insist you at least let us get you to a place of safety." She looked at them seriously. "I don't want to frighten you, but you really are in a tight spot. We're very vulnerable out in the open like this."

John swore under his breath. "They've spotted us."

"Rand," Nicole said, her eyes wide. "Look. The men who were watching my apartment just crossed the street."

"More company at the east end, Marsha," John informed her, pointing that way and grabbing Nicole by the arm.

Rand swiveled his head. At one end of the grocery store parking lot the car with the supposed Russian agents was headed their way. At the other end a blue sedan with a battered trunk was also closing fast. He looked at Marsha.

"Well, Toadstool?" she asked.

"Let's go!" They all dashed for the car Marsha indicated. "But if you call me Toadstool one more time, I'm going to take back what I said about your legs."

CHAPTER ELEVEN

John was a better driver than Rand, Nicole, and the people after them combined. Like a ferret in a tunnel, he wound so expertly through the Denver streets that even a native like Nicole wasn't sure where they would emerge.

But emerge they did, at a brand-new, immaculately landscaped office park on the south side of the city. John parked the car in an underground lot beneath one soaring edifice of glass and steel, and they rode the elevator up to what Marsha called their temporary operational headquarters. It was a pleasant group of rooms, with modern furnishings and plenty of light from the broad picture windows looking out on the mountains in the distance.

"Your agency must be well funded," Rand remarked.

"We use new buildings like this for field operations quite often," Marsha explained, "when the owners are hungry for tenants and we can get special rates."

Another thing that seemed rather odd was that

there were no other agents around, but they were assured that it was standard procedure for an operation of such a delicate nature. Marsha led them into a meeting room dominated by a long, highly polished table that had comfortable leather chairs situated around its perimeter.

While John got everybody coffee, Marsha busied herself setting up a rather complicated-looking tape recorder at the opposite end of the table. It was all very official and professional, yet with an underlying current of urgency, and when the female agent pointed a pair of microphones in their direction, Rand and Nicole started to get nervous again. The symmetrical blooms of fresh-cut, gaily colored freesia in vases scattered around the room was a comforting touch.

When they were all seated and had their coffee, Marsha started the proceedings. "This is Marsha, code five," she said in a clear voice.

"And John, code fifty-five," her partner added.

"In the matter of the Netherlands tape," Marsha continued. "State your names and occupations, please."

After a nervous glance at Nicole, Rand did so. "Rand Jameson, wholesale florist. And I'd like to take this opportunity to say we haven't done anything wrong."

"Nicole Sabine, grower and wholesaler of fine cut flowers. And I'd feel a lot better if you would show us some identification now," Nicole told them.

"Surely you must realize we don't carry it in

the field? We're not police officers, nor are we from any bureau or security force you'd recognize. We're undercover agents. And I'm afraid I'm not really at liberty to divulge our position with the government, in any case."

"It seems we have a quandary," Rand observed.

"Not really." Marsha fixed them with a serious gaze. "Either you trust us or you don't."

"And if we don't?" Nicole wanted to know.

Marsha sighed. "In that case things could get messy."

"Are you threatening us?"

"I am simply telling you the realities of the situation, Nicole," she replied sharply. "What we have here is an international incident in the making. As you have seen firsthand, there are a lot of people who want that tape. Foreign governments, free-lance operatives working for the highest bidder, even bad seeds from intelligence agencies right here in our own country."

"Don't forget Lieutenant Koslyn," Rand put in wryly.

Marsha nodded. "We're aware of him, as well as an informant of his in New York, a Customs official whom we've had under surveillance for some time. Koslyn, I'm afraid, has fallen into the hands of a group of Federal agents, the bad seeds I just told you about," she informed them, though she didn't seem overly concerned about the rogue detective's welfare.

"The three men in the blue sedan?" Nicole inquired.

"That's right. I doubt Koslyn is enjoying his stay with them," Marsha said. "It is a fate that could easily befall you if you don't cooperate with us."

"Now that," Rand observed, "really does sound like a threat. Are you saying you'll hand us over to them if we don't do as you say?"

"No!" Marsha answered vehemently. "What I'm saying is that we have a real jurisdictional quagmire here. In theory, all of the people from our government who are after you have the power of the law behind them. In fact, however, a good number of them are abusing that power for monetary gain. One of our assigned tasks is to root those rotten apples out of the government barrel, but until we can do so, they have as much right to detain you for questioning as we do."

"That's why you let us run around loose?" Nicole asked. "To find out who has dirty hands, so to speak?"

The other woman nodded. "That's right. In fact, we're not even sure who we can depend on in our own agency," she told them, her tone ominous. "This mess runs that deep. The only way you're going to be safe is by ending it right here and now. You'll have all the proof you need that we're the good guys by the way your lives return to normal after you give us that tape."

"Lord," Nicole moaned, rubbing her temples. "Normal. How nice that sounds." She looked at

Rand. He seemed just as confused as she felt. "What should we do?"

Rand frowned. "What is on the tape?" he asked Marsha.

"I can't tell you that!" she exclaimed incredulously.

"How can you honestly expect us to trust you if you don't trust us?" he pressed. "We're in this up to our necks already. Don't you think you owe us some kind of explanation after all we've been through?"

Marsha returned to her seat. She sat there, pondering the problem for a full minute before finally nodding her head. "All right. You see, Rand, the tape is ours."

"Ours? You mean America's?"

"Yes. I can't tell you what's on it, but undoubtedly you've surmised that it is of a strategic nature. It was originated by one of our deep-cover agents, relayed around Europe, and ended up in your flower shipment," she explained. "It was bound for another operative of ours at JFK, and from there it would have found its way directly to the White House."

"What went wrong?" Nicole asked.

John chuckled tersely. "To be quite blunt, you two are what went wrong."

The pair looked at each other nervously. "Us?" they asked in unison.

"The flower route had served us well. It was quick, efficient, and relatively inexpensive as these things go. We called it the Gladiola Connection."

Nicole frowned. "We found the tube with the tape in it in a bunch of glads, all right. But why did someone tear up the auratum lilies?"

"That would be our friends in the blue sedan," Marsha answered. "How they found out about our shipment, we've yet to ascertain, but their informant obviously didn't know all the particulars." She chuckled and smiled. "You'll be reimbursed for the damage they did, by the way. I saw it firsthand, by pretending to be a reporter and snooping around. It was horrible what they did to such pretty flowers."

"Marsha," Nicole said, "you are a woman after my own heart. I'll believe anyone who tells me to send them a bill."

"I'm starting to feel trusting already," Rand agreed.

"I met Orchid face-to-face too. What do you call him? Vin? He's quite the character, Nicole. Even though he threw me off the property, I like him." Marsha looked at Rand and winked. "Perhaps because he commented on my legs too."

John cleared his throat and looked at them pointedly. "Getting back to whose fault it was," he said, "the whole thing fell apart when you two juggled brokers. Our man at the airport lost track of the shipment, and by the time he found out what had happened, it was already gone."

"So," Marsha said, her smile fading and her voice suddenly turning businesslike once again, "there you have it, or as much of it as you're going to get from us, at any rate. It has been helpful following you around, seeing who else took an interest in you, and I must say I am impressed by your patriotism in putting yourselves at risk like this." She cleared her throat and looked at them, one eyebrow raised. "Even if you did bring it all on your own heads."

Nicole looked at Rand. "I think we've just been told that we're fine citizens but sort of dumb."

"Talk about a backhanded compliment," he said, agreeing.

"However," Marsha continued, "the time has come for you to do your duty. We must have that tape, and we must have it now."

"It's in a safe place," Nicole assured them. She smiled at Rand, taking his hand and searching his eyes. "I think this is finally over. What do you think?"

He squeezed her hand. "I'm not sure, Nicole."

Rand didn't know what to think. These two people seemed to be exactly what they had been looking for. Maybe that was the problem. They seemed almost too right, as if they had been listening when Rand had outlined what he thought the good guys would be like.

But there was something else troubling him, something that eclipsed the problem of what to do with the tape. It was quite obvious by the relieved look in her eyes that Nicole desperately wanted to put an end to this. He did, too, and yet, in a way it was the last thing he wanted—because he was in love with her and didn't know if she felt the same way about him or not.

In spite of the danger, ending this time together would give her the opportunity to think things over. When Nicole spoke of putting an end to this, did she mean the horrible muddle they had gotten themselves into, or everything? They had shared so much, and yet it had been forced upon them. What would happen when their lives returned to normal?

"Rand?" She was looking at him questioningly.

"There are a couple of things that will have to happen before I turn the tape over to you," he told the two agents.

"And they are?" Marsha asked.

"Turn off that tape recorder first," he demanded, watching warily until she had done so.

The tension in the room was thick. "All right, Jameson," John said curtly. "What's on your mind?"

"One, you are going to let us walk out of here right now. I'll give you the tape at a time and place of my own choosing," Rand informed them. Nicole grabbed his arm and started to object, but he cut her off. "Two, when you come to the meeting, you will bring one hundred thousand dollars in unmarked bills with random serial numbers."

Nicole chuckled nervously. "He's kidding,"

she assured Marsha and John. "Tell them you're kidding, Rand."

"I'm quite serious. You'll never get that tape unless you do just as I say."

"Are you insane?" Nicole cried, jumping to her feet and glaring at him. "I don't know what this is all about, Rand, but I'm not playing along this time." Had he been lying to her all along? What kind of man had she lost her heart to? "It's over. If you won't give them the tape, I will."

"Don't listen to her, Marsha," he said. "She doesn't know where the tape is. I hid it when she wasn't watching."

Nicole groaned and sank back into her chair. He was right. And it all made sense now. Their whole time together had been a lie, just Rand's way of keeping the opposition confused until all the sharks had gathered. He hadn't been looking for good guys, he'd been looking for the people to whom the tape belonged, the ripest pickings.

John and Marsha, however, didn't seem the least bit surprised. Angry but not surprised. "We were prepared for this contingency," Marsha admitted, "although we thought we'd be buying the tape from whoever caught and killed you to get it, not you. That could still come to pass if you insist on playing this game. There are some nasty people out there, Jameson."

"I've done okay so far," he said, his tone and manner nonchalant. "I'm sure we'll be fine for the time it takes to get the tape and make the exchange."

"Do you realize that what you're doing is treason?"

"Come on." Rand laughed derisively. "I've figured you two out. If you were really who you say you are, we'd be sweating through an interrogation right now."

John sighed. "I told you the goody-two-shoes routine wouldn't work, Marsha. We should have roughed them up." His eyes took on an evil gleam. "Maybe we still should. Even if we killed them getting the information, we could make it look like the Russians did it."

"No." She was looking at Rand and Nicole appraisingly. "There would be suspicions from higher up. The setup is too sweet to risk blowing our cover over a hundred grand."

"You mean you . . ." Nicole stared at them, eyes wide. She was so confused now, she couldn't get her mouth to work. "You really are the bad guys?"

Marsha chuckled. "My goodness! You really are naïve, aren't you?" She turned her attention to Rand. "All right, Jameson. You win. You're a pretty sharp cookie."

"Sharp enough to know a liar when I see one."

"Oh, everything I told you was the truth," she said. "Except for what we plan to do with the tape."

"Who are you going to sell it to?"

Marsha laughed. "Better quit while you're ahead, Rand. Now here's the deal. You get the tape, arrange the meeting however you want.

We're going to file a report that the tape was accidentally destroyed, so I suggest you make it somewhere you don't mind seeing go up in flames. And don't get greedy," she warned. "It's worth a hundred thousand to us to do this the easy way but not much more. You'll have your money and your health; we'll sell the tape, make a profit, and still keep our positions with the agency."

"But won't your superiors realize that the information on the tape is in circulation?" Rand wanted to know.

Marsha shook her head. "That doesn't concern you. Suffice it to say it's the sort of data that's hot today, cold tomorrow. We're selling it at its hottest. Unless there's a war, it won't make much difference who has it."

"Traitors!" Nicole cried. She pointed at Rand. "You too! All of you!"

"Your girlfriend sounds like she could present a problem," John observed. "Maybe she should get caught in the fire too."

Rand stiffened. "Make another threat like that and you'll never get the tape." He put his hand on Nicole's shoulder. "She'll come around when she sees the money," he assured them. He winked at her and added, "She just watches too much television, that's all."

Nicole stared at him. She opened her mouth, then closed it again, a bewildered look on her face. "I could use fifty thousand dollars," she managed to say at last, her eyes never leaving Rand's.

"That's more like it," Marsha said. "Everybody can come out of this richer if we just take it easy and keep our mouths shut. John, give Rand the keys to your car. We'll use mine to go to the meeting when he calls." She took a piece of paper and wrote down the phone number for him. "We'll be waiting, Rand. Call when you're ready, but make it soon."

Rand took Nicole by the hand, pocketed the number Marsha gave him, and grabbed the keys to John's car. He strode toward the door, Nicole in tow. "You'll hear from us tomorrow morning."

"At the latest," Marsha said, pointing a warning finger at him. "Don't get cute, Jameson. Like I said earlier, in this game a little knowledge can be a dangerous thing."

"Deadly, in fact," John agreed.

When Nicole and Rand had gone, Marsha looked at her partner. "Well. That took an interesting turn."

"Didn't it, though. I must say you handled yourself pretty well, coming back as quick as you please with that bit about being prepared for every contingency," John said appreciatively. "Makes me proud to be associated with you. A hundred grand! Do you think they bought it?"

She shrugged. "With those two, who knows? They're just full of surprises. Doesn't matter much one way or the other, though," Marsha added, grinning broadly. "We really are prepared for every contingency."

They got up and went to the window, waiting impatiently until they saw John's car emerge from the underground parking area with Rand at the wheel and Nicole beside him. Marsha pulled a black box out of her purse and flipped a switch. The homing signal was coming in loud and clear.

"Is it working?" John asked anxiously.

"Perfectly," Marsha assured him. "We'll be able to track them wherever they go, as long as we don't get more than ten miles away from them."

He rubbed his hands together in anticipation. "Then the tape will soon be ours. I'll go get the other car."

"Right. I'll meet you out front." She heard John hurry out the door but kept watching as Rand and Nicole pulled away from the building. "Sorry, you two," the woman calling herself Marsha murmured. "But at least you were right about one thing: You can't trust anyone these days."

CHAPTER TWELVE

"Nicole—"

She pushed his hand away. "There's just one thing I want to know, Rand. Are you going to break your promise?"

"No!" His reply had been a reflex, then he asked, "What promise?"

"I thought as much. Your promise to look after me, that you would never do anything to hurt me. It was just as much a lie as everything else you've done or said, wasn't it?"

Rand had learned a few tricks from the agent John. He was using them now as they headed for the cabin by a wildly unpredictable route. But her accusation hit him so hard, he had to slow down and glance at her.

"You're not actually telling me you believe . . ." He trailed off and started laughing. "I must be one heck of an actor! Maybe I should quit the wholesale business and move to Hollywood."

Nicole glared at him. "Not this time, Rand," she bit out through clenched teeth. She had made a vow to herself not to cry but didn't know if she could keep it. "I'm not falling for another of your stories."

"That does it," Rand grumbled, pulling over to the side of the road. When the car had stopped, he turned and glared at her. "I've had it up to here with your suspicions and accusations. I am not a spy, Nicole. Nor am I a smuggler or an extortionist, and I am most certainly not a traitor!" he informed her, wild-eyed with outrage.

"Hah!"

Rand's face was turning red. "Why, you . . . I could just throttle you!"

"Go ahead," Nicole told him. "That's probably next in your plans, anyway, isn't it?"

He grabbed the wheel instead of her throat, his knuckles turning white. "Did I or did I not just get us away from two rogue intelligence agents?"

She frowned. "Well, yes, but—"

"To whom you were about to give the tape cheerfully?"

"Okay, so you're smarter than I am," she replied petulantly. "That still doesn't mean I believe you made a deal with them just to get us out of there. You realized they were dirty and saw your opportunity to make a bundle."

"Damn!" Rand slammed the car in gear and pulled onto the road, spraying gravel everywhere. Then, narrowly avoiding a collision, he whipped the wheel around and turned across traffic to head back the way they had come. "We'll just return to that office and offer to take them to the tape for free. Will that satisfy you?"

"They'll kill us!"

"Then at least we'll die with you knowing I wasn't a traitor," he said bitterly.

Nicole had pressed herself against the door away from him. "You really are crazy! Turn this car around, Rand. We can't go back there now. I . . . I won't say anything to anyone," she vowed, petrified by the wild light in his eyes. "You can have all the money, and I'll keep quiet about this whole thing."

"I don't want the money!" he yelled. "Would you get that into your thick skull? All I want is your trust." And your love, he thought, but he knew she wouldn't believe that, either. "I just didn't feel right about those two. There was something too friendly about them. The only way I could think of to prove that they were on the take and get out of there with our skins was to make a deal for the tape."

She was looking at him doubtfully. Her whole world had been so confused and upset the last few days, she was no longer sure if she even trusted herself, let alone anyone else. John and Marsha hadn't seemed quite right to her, either, but she had been so anxious to be done with this mess that she hardly cared what happened to the tape anymore.

"What were you going to do after we got away?" Nicole asked. "They won't be happy with you for deceiving them, you know."

Rand sighed forlornly. "Lord, I don't know. I hadn't thought that far ahead." He glanced at her. "I was hoping you would help me figure it out. The only plan I had . . ." He trailed off, wondering how she would take his explanation of the real reasons he had begun this subterfuge.

"Go on," she prompted. "What was your plan?"

"I'll be honest with you," he replied hesitantly. "I don't really give a damn about the tape anymore. All this intrigue, spies, and danger for a little strip of tape. It's insane! Let the government handle it. I just want an end to it, no matter how it turns out. I'm tired."

He looked tired. Nicole knew she looked the same way; she felt even worse. "That's all I want, too, Rand," she told him quietly. "I want it to be over. I mean, it's been fun in a way, but—"

"You see? That's what I'm trying to tell you. I want this strange muddle we're in to be over, but I've enjoyed it in a way, too, and . . ." Rand couldn't seem to get the words out. "Making a deal with them was also a way I could extend this a little longer so we could . . ."

"Would you spit it out?" Nicole demanded suspiciously.

"What do you mean when you say you want it over?"

"Over. Finished. I want to be a normal person again," she replied. "What do you mean?"

"What kind of normal?"

"Just normal! What are you driving at?"

"I want—"

Nicole grabbed his arm and interrupted him.

"Rand! Isn't that John and Marsha in that car coming this way?"

"What?" He looked, swiveling his head as the car went past, going in the opposite direction. "It sure looked like them," he muttered, almost glad for the reprieve. Talking about his feelings had never been easy for him. "But they're not turning around, even though they must have seen us as well. If they're tailing us, wouldn't they be on our backs by now?"

Nicole watched as the car with the two agents inside disappeared behind them. "Maybe," she said thoughtfully. "And maybe not. We must have had a pretty good head start on them, and we did so much twisting and turning that I almost got carsick. Yet there they were, like shadows only a few miles behind us."

"Do you watch those detective brothers on television?" Rand asked suddenly, his eyes widening.

"I watch too much television, remember?" she replied. "And I saw that episode. Stop the car!"

Tires screeching, Rand turned off the road and onto a side street. They both got out of the car and started going over it from bumper to bumper, Rand flat on his back and peering beneath the vehicle while Nicole felt around under the fenders. Their antics started to draw a curious, if wary, crowd of children.

"What does a homing beacon look like?" Nicole asked.

"How should I know? Just keep looking."

A young boy got brave enough to approach them. "What are you looking for, mister? Did you hit a skunk or something?"

"Go away kid," Rand muttered.

"No, son," Nicole told him. "We didn't hit a skunk."

The youth seemed disappointed. "Oh." He started to walk away, then his face brightened. "Hey! You're looking for a bomb! Hey, everybody!" he announced to the growing crowd. "Their car's going to blow up!"

The onlookers gasped. One little girl ran to tell her mother. Most, however, were just as stouthearted as the boy, who was still standing over Rand as he wiggled around beneath the car. The boy bent over for a better look. The top scoop of his triple-decker ice-cream cone fell right on Rand's stomach.

"Our car is *not* going to blow up!" Rand insisted, removing the ice cream from his shirt with distaste. "Don't I hear your mother calling you?"

"Got it!" Nicole cried triumphantly.

She pulled a small metal box from beneath the left rear fender. Rand got up, glared at his young tormentor as he brushed his clothes off, then went to Nicole's side.

"Sure looks like one," he agreed, frowning. "I guess."

"What should we do with it now?" she asked.

Rand smiled wickedly. "How about sticking it on some other car? That should confuse John and Marsha."

"It would," Nicole agreed, "but they're a dangerous pair. We don't want to get some innocent bystander in trouble, Rand."

"No." He thought for a moment, then looked at the young boy, who was presently smearing his ice cream all over their windshield. "Hey, kid!"

"Yeah?"

"Is there a coffee shop around here?"

The boy pointed down the street, stuck the remainder of his ice-cream cone on the hood of the car like an ornament, then took off running. But Rand was too caught up in his idea to be angry. He ushered Nicole into the car, got in himself, then started the engine and took off in the direction in which the boy had pointed.

At the coffee shop Rand found just the vehicle he was looking for. It took him only a moment to attach the homing device to the fender of the black-and-white car, then he once again got them back on the road toward the cabin.

"That ought to confuse them, all right," Nicole said, barely containing her laughter.

"Can't you just picture the look on John and Marsha's faces when they find out they're following a police cruiser?"

They drove on, occasionally doubling back or waiting by the side of the road hidden among the pine trees, just to make certain they had lost the two agents tailing them. It was getting dark by the time they neared their safe haven, the cozy cabin belonging to Rand's friend, Jim.

In all the excitement Nicole had forgotten to

be mad at Rand. How could she stay mad at him? He had outwitted the two agents by making a deal with them, thus proving they were rotten, and then had been prepared to walk right back into their clutches just to prove to her that he hadn't really intended to sell the tape.

But he obviously had something on his mind, something he couldn't seem to put into words. Evidently it had to do with what would happen when all this was over. Knowing that, Nicole wasn't in any particular hurry to find out what it was. He was probably trying to tell her that he wanted to return to normal, too; normal as in getting back to work, forgetting what had happened to them, and especially forgetting what had happened *between* them.

Maybe he wanted out. They had been forced together, right into each other's arms, as a matter of fact. Perhaps Rand had come to the same conclusion she had—it all had happened too fast. The intimacy they had shared might never have happened at all if not for the intrigue and danger surrounding them. Rand wanted to tell her it had been fun, but that was all.

And yet, she thought as she watched him drive the car up the bumpy drive to the cabin, hadn't he also mentioned something about wanting to extend the time between them? Hadn't he implied that an underlying reason for making a deal with Marsha and John was to give them a little more time together?

Of course. He wanted time, all right, the kind

of dangerous time they both admitted they enjoyed, that seemed to make their lovemaking all the sweeter. The thought made Nicole angry for a moment, but when the cabin came into view in the rosy glow of sunset, she had a change of heart.

They were safe for the moment again. They would make plans, figure out the best way to get the tape off their hands. But they would have hours to spare until the morning deadline. Afterward, no matter who got the tape, everything would return to normal. This would be their last night. This might be the last time they made love.

"Rand," Nicole murmured, putting her hand on his thigh as he parked among the trees. "That discussion we were having earlier, about what's going to happen when this is over—"

"Let's get settled first," he said, interrupting quickly. "We have other things to get out of the way, plans to make and so on."

She nodded. "I agree."

"You do?" He looked at her, surprised. "Does that mean you've decided to believe I'm not going to sell the tape, that I'm not a traitor?"

"Yes." She kissed him on the cheek. "I'm sorry for doubting you. My world has been turned upside down," she explained, wanting to tell him that most of her confusion came from the love she felt, a love she couldn't speak of. "I guess I was having trouble seeing clearly. Again."

Rand chuckled and pulled her close, his lips

finding hers unerringly in the twilight. He wanted her so badly, he thought he might burst.

"I know what you mean. I've never been in . . ." He couldn't say it. How would she react? Maybe later, after they had talked things over. "I've never been in a situation like this before, either," he completed. "Come on. Let's get inside."

"Yes."

The cabin was as they had left it, small yet inviting, filled with the memory of the delights they had shared the previous night. They both felt it, found themselves looking into each other's eyes and then away, an unspoken communication of the sensuality they felt smoldering within.

"This is where I hid the tape," Rand said, pointing to a spot on the mantel above the stone fireplace. "The mantel is loose here, and there's just enough room to slide the tube between it and the stone. See?" He motioned for her to look.

Nicole barely glanced at the tape. "I told you I trust you, Rand." *With everything but my heart.* But that was gone already, so why fight it? She wanted him one last time, before he returned to the free life he had led before they had been thrust together. "Let's figure out what we're going to do with the stupid thing. I want to go to bed."

"How could you possibly be sleepy?" he wanted to know. "My nerves are jumping like live wires."

"So are mine." She rubbed against him. "I didn't say I was sleepy."

Rand's eyes opened wide. He felt a stirring within him, a powerful desire tempered by the tenderness that seized him every time he looked at her.

"Oh," he managed to say, his voice husky. "I know exactly what you mean."

"As a matter of fact," she murmured, her voice a purr as she took him by the hand and led the way into the bedroom, "let's postpone the discussion until much, much later."

Nicole undressed him with petal-soft hands, her movements slow and teasing as she did the same for herself before lowering herself to the downy bed. She beckoned to him, and he joined her, his mind reeling at her sensuous, inviting beauty.

"Nicole . . ."

She shook her head and smiled, then kissed him, glorying in his throaty moan as she tenderly took his lower lip between her own and caressed him with her tongue. Rand's body came alive, and he was suddenly stroking her everywhere at once, caressing her sweet, hard-tipped breasts, her smooth thighs, the delight of her sweet femininity.

"Make love to me, Rand," she whispered in his ear, nibbling delicately on the lobe. "I need you."

He suckled her gently, pulling first one dusky pink nipple into his mouth and then the other, feeling her move beneath him in ecstasy. Nipping at her softly rounded belly with his teeth, his head dipped still lower, probing, tasting as she writhed at his intimate touch, her breathless moans taunting him until neither of them could stand any more.

"Now, please," she said with a moan. "I want to feel you inside me."

"You will," he promised, needing no further prompting. "All of me, my sweet Nicole."

The bloom of her desire opened for him, held him, grasping at his hard, powerful masculinity as he tenderly made them one. Their tongues dancing in each other's mouths, they drank of each other, drawing every ounce of pleasure from the union of love they shared.

It wasn't like the first time, with the desperate need they had felt, nor like any time thereafter. They understood each other better now, all the small movements and tender, urgent, yet unspoken directions. This time they gave and received as equals, the gentle taking turns with the strong, rolling, twisting, and flowing to a powerful culmination.

Then they returned from their mindless, passionate journey, savoring each drop of their desire, like flowers lifting their petals to the heavens for life-giving water. Like flowers, too, nurtured by rich soil, Nicole and Rand felt nurtured in each other's arms. Some emotion within them had grown deep, spreading roots, holding them together, binding them so tightly that they would forever be as branches of the same stem.

Rand rested at Nicole's side, watching the afterglow settle over her skin, devouring her beauty. She was so lovely. He loved the way she looked at him, her eyes gliding over his face and body as if memorizing his every feature. Was he deluding himself, or did he see his love returned in those pale gray-green pools?

The time had come to find out. "I'm sorry, Nicole."

"For what?" Here it comes, she thought. She turned away, willing the tears not to flow from her eyes. "You were fantastic." As always. And she wanted to remember him just as he was right now, forever.

Rand wrapped his arm around her, pulling her tightly against him. "That's not what I meant, you silly wench," he told her playfully. "I meant I was sorry for doing this to you. It's so selfish—"

"No." Nicole put her finger to his lips to silence him. "It wasn't selfish at all. I wanted it as well, very much," she assured him, forcing herself to look into his eyes again. He had to understand. "I figured out what you were trying to say earlier. You didn't really mean you didn't care who got the tape."

He smiled. "That's right. It's just that there was something else more important to me." Rand cupped her face with one of his big, strong hands. "I'm sorry because I had other motives for making the deal with those bad apples. I knew it would give us time. Time for this." He kissed her softly, tracing her lips with the tip of his tongue. "And it was selfish."

Nicole shook her head. "How could it be? Soon this will come to an end. I wanted you one last time too."

"Yes." Now Rand averted his gaze, unable to look at her face. One last time. So it was true. She wanted everything to end, the danger as well as the passion they had shared. Then he frowned. "Wait a minute. Did you say *too?* As in *also?*"

"What?"

"You said you wanted me one last time *too.* As if that's all I wanted."

"Isn't it?"

Rand looked at the bewildered expression on her face, knowing it to be mirrored on his own. "Finally I get to ask you if you're insane. When I said I wasn't ready for the end of this mess, I meant I didn't want to give you time to think before I could convince you."

"Convince me of what?" Nicole asked, totally befuddled.

"To fall in love with me too," he replied. "I realized that once the tape was gone, you would want to return to the way things were before."

"Of course I do, but—"

"You said you wanted it over. Everything. You told me that you wanted to go back to business as usual, including our rivalry. I thought you wanted me out of your life."

"What?" she cried. "Hold on a minute. You said it too."

Rand looked at her as if she'd lost her mind. Wasn't this hard enough already? "Excuse me?"

"Too. As in *also*. You said you wanted to convince me to love you *too*."

"Right." He nodded, frowning in confusion. "I had hoped this time would let me do that. But then you started talking about one last—"

Nicole put her hand over his mouth. "Would you shut up? All along we've been living scenes from television and movies, and I feel like I'm stuck in one now." She glared at him fiercely. "Tell me exactly what you want to tell me!"

"I . . ."

"Well?"

Rand stroked her cheek with his thumb. "I love you, Nicole. I started out as your rival, maybe not hating you but pretty close, then somewhere along the way I started wanting you, then liking you, and I finally fell in love with you. At first I thought it was just the excitement—"

"So did I," she said, interrupting softly. "It was the same for me. I did hate you, for being so sharp at importing and taking money out of my pocket. Then we met, and this happened to us, and . . . now you've got me doing it!" she exclaimed, cross with herself. "I love you, Rand. And it didn't happen just now, either. Somewhere along the way I simply fell in love."

Rand felt as if he were in a dream. "Then what's all this about one last time?" he asked incredulously.

"You tell me!"

"I didn't say it!" he objected. "You did."

Chills were running up and down Nicole's spine, while at the same time she felt warm from head to toe. "I was being kind, you ungrateful wretch. I thought you wanted to return to your old life, a freewheeling businessman with a woman on each arm."

"Me?" He laughed uproariously. "Me? I've been too busy staying ahead of the competition even to date. One of the things I liked about this situation we got caught up in is that it was like one long, crazy date with the woman of my dreams." Then Rand grabbed her and hugged her. "Not to mention the fact that I needed the exercise."

"You rat!"

"I love you, Nicole," he whispered in her ear.

"I love you, Rand," she murmured, softening in his arms. Then she came to her senses and started thumping him on the back. "But you're still a rat!"

Rand pinned her hands to her sides. "What did I do?"

"You were going to seduce me again, that's what. There I was, thinking you wanted to go back to your bachelor ways, ready to offer myself to you one final time—"

"Because you loved me," he interjected, unable to get enough of the sound of the words.

"Because I loved you," she continued, "and there you were, making a deal with those creeps so you could get me alone again, planning all along to seduce me—"

"Because I loved you." He couldn't get enough of saying it, either.

She nodded impatiently. "Because you loved me and—"

Rand kissed her firmly to quiet her. "And always will love you. I want to marry you, I want you to have my children, and I want them to all grow up knowing all about flowers, growing and selling the finest flowers in the world."

"Oh, Rand," she said, her voice little more than a sigh. "Let's not talk about that now. I'm having enough trouble getting used to the idea of being in love."

He stiffened and drew back to look at her face. "I've just proposed to you, Nicole. I'll admit it wasn't something I ever imagined myself doing before all this started, but now that I have, I feel obliged to press for an answer."

"Rand . . ." Wasn't this what she wanted—had dreamed of, in fact? "Everything has been happening so fast. I—I can't give you an answer, not right now, not while we're still under all this pressure. I need time—"

"Time to think?" he said, completing her thought, his voice an ominous whisper.

She loved him. He loved her. Why was there still so much confusion in her mind? "Well, yes, but not in the way you mean."

"Oh, really?" Rand pulled away from her, pushing himself off the bed to a standing position.

He started getting dressed. "Don't you see that this is exactly what I was afraid of, Nicole? I know what you want. You want to return to the bosom of your family, a family that hates my guts."

Nicole got out of bed and put on her clothes, too, then faced him angrily. "They do not hate you!" she objected. "They just don't trust you. I love you, Rand. But you have to admit that one week—even a week that has seemed to last a year —is hardly enough time to start making decisions about marriage and children and raising them in the flower business!"

"It is for me," Rand informed her.

"There are so many things to consider," she continued, the implications of the situation suddenly hitting her. "There's Vin. He's so proud. He thinks of me as the heir to the business. It will take him awhile to get used to the idea of me marrying and changing my name, especially to that of a former rival."

Rand blew out an angry breath. "So we'll hypenate our names or something!" he exclaimed.

She barely heard him. "You haven't even met my father yet. In some ways he's worse than Vin. And he most definitely thinks of me as a daughter, with all the protective instincts that relationship brings about." Nicole sat down on the bed, putting her face in her hands. "Lord! The problems!"

"We'll work them out, Nicole. All that matters is that we love each other."

"Are we even sure of that, Rand?" she asked desperately. "You said yourself that at first you thought it was just the excitement, the way we were thrown together."

"At first, yes. But not now. I love you, Nicole, with all my heart," he said, looking intently into her eyes. "Do you feel the same way or not?"

"I do, but—"

"Then what are you afraid of?" he demanded.

"Stop pressuring me!" she cried. "I need time to think things through, that's all."

Rand took her by the arms. "Do you know what I'm afraid of, Nicole? I'm afraid that once this is over, once you're back in the safe nest of your family and submerged in your work again, you'll convince yourself it's best for Sabine if you never see me again."

"I will not!" she objected vehemently. "And if I do, maybe it is for the best. If our love can't stand up to a little time and a more normal relationship, maybe it isn't real at all!"

"I knew it!" They were standing toe-to-toe, glowering at each other. Rand was beside himself with a confusing mixture of love, anger, and desperation. "Nicole—"

"Ssh!" She frowned. "What was that noise?"

"You're not getting out of this so easily, Nicole," he shot back. "No noise is going to save you. I want an answer and I want it right now."

Nicole waved her hand for silence. "I'm serious. I heard something." She wrapped her arms around him. "There it was again!"

"I don't hear . . ." But there was something. He held Nicole close. "Maybe the raccoons?"

"Not unless they wear shoes," Nicole said, her voice quavering. "Footsteps! They've found us, Rand!"

The front door crashed open. Rand and Nicole practically jumped out of their skins. Then they smelled a rank odor and realized that the uninvited visitor was much, much worse than John and Marsha. With Rand in front, they crept to the bedroom door and peered out into the living area.

"I'm not at all happy with you two," Koslyn informed them through a thick cloud of foul cigar smoke. The rough quality of his voice was matched by the fury in his muddy brown eyes. His gun was in his hand, and it was pointing right at them. "No, I'm not happy at all."

CHAPTER THIRTEEN

"Well, isn't this cozy," Koslyn rasped as he looked around the cabin. "A little love nest. It's not much, but it's one heck of a lot better than the pit I've spent the last twenty-four hours in."

"Look, Koslyn—"

"Shut up, buddy boy." He aimed the gun right between Rand's eyes. "I suppose you really laughed it up when those three goons grabbed me, didn't you?" he asked bitterly.

"If it makes you feel any better," Nicole said, bravely stepping out from behind Rand, "it ruined our night as well as yours. And believe me, we weren't laughing. We've had a tough time of it too."

"Compared to what I've got in store for you, lady," Koslyn promised, "it'll seem like a picnic."

Rand's fists clenched at his sides. "Let us explain."

"I told you to shut up. You'll pay, both of you, as well that old idiot who rammed us on the freeway, me bouncing around in the backseat like a Ping-Pong ball." His horrible grimace grew even worse at the memory. "But the worst part was that it was all for nothing. A fake tape. Those guys just about shot my kneecaps off when they found out it was bogus, and I had one devil of a time convincing them to let me go so I could track you down and get the real one."

It was obvious there was no use bargaining with the man. Perhaps if they made him mad enough, he'd make a careless mistake. Rand sneered at him.

"You deserved that and more, Koslyn. You wouldn't have taken our word that we didn't know what was going on, would you?" he asked. "We had to trick you so we could follow you and find out who you took the tape to, maybe discover who really owned it."

Koslyn took the cigar out of his mouth and spit on the floor. "Patriots. You make me sick. I don't care what you wanted to do. All I know is that you owe me, Jameson. Now hand over that tape." He waved his gun threateningly. "The genuine article this time."

"On one condition," Rand told him, figuring he didn't have much to lose by trying. "If we do, you go away and leave us alone."

Koslyn laughed, an awful, rasping sound. "Go away? Sure. I'll go away, but not until I've evened the score against you dirty double-crossers."

"Then no deal."

He stepped closer to Rand, his eyes gleaming

with hatred. "We're not making deals here, Jameson."

"No?" Rand managed a curt laugh, hoping it sounded convincing. "In that case, why should I tell you anything? What's in it for us?"

The beefy man grinned, showing his stained teeth. "A quick end. You don't want your lady friend there to suffer, do you?"

Rand had to use every bit of willpower he had not to grab Koslyn by the throat. "You're going to have to make a decision, Koslyn. Revenge or the tape."

"I'm a cop, remember? Don't you think I know how to search a place?"

Nicole was so frightened, she could barely move, but she had to get his attention away from Rand. "It's not in here," she informed him, grasping at straws.

Rand's eyes widened. "That's right. It's out there," he said, pointing out the open door, "hidden in a hollow tree. There's only a few thousand of them in the forest. Shouldn't take you more than a month or so to find the right one."

"Show me," he demanded, aiming the gun at Nicole.

"Why?" Nicole asked sarcastically. "You're going to shoot us, in any case. And the longer you play around here, the more chance that the two spies we arranged to sell the tape to will show up."

Rand looked at her. If he could, he would have thrown his arms around her and given her a big hug. "That's right. We were forced to make a deal with a couple of agents on the take, a real nasty pair you'd probably get along with just fine, Koslyn," Rand said, picking up the story. "A hundred grand. How about you?"

"A hundred grand?" Avarice shone in Koslyn's eyes. "I made a deal with those three goons for half that. Of course, they told me they'd track me down like a dog if I crossed them, but that much dough can hide a guy pretty good."

He didn't notice the secretive smile Nicole gave Rand. "How about it, Koslyn?" she asked. "Feel like dealing now? We can give you the whole setup. You can make the deal with the spies and keep the money. All you have to do is agree to let us go."

Koslyn stared at them. Evidently he hated them a great deal, because it took him a moment before greed won out over his need for revenge. "All right. Let's assume for a moment that I'm stupid enough to believe you'll take me to the tape and that you're stupid enough to think I won't shoot you afterward. What's your plan?"

"Listen, Koslyn," Rand interjected. "We're getting to know each other pretty well by now, right? You know the kind of people we are, and we know the kind of man you are."

"So?"

"We made the deal with the agents, but we never planned on going through with it. We're patriots, remember? But we're tired."

"I've heard this one before," the other man muttered.

"And we've fallen in love," Nicole added, putting her arm around Rand. "We want a normal life, that's all. We know you despise us. What kind of life would we have if we double-crossed you again, knowing you'd come after us?"

Koslyn sneered. "Isn't that sweet? But you'd better believe I'd come after you."

"We know. That's why you can trust us."

"Maybe," he admitted doubtfully. "The plan, Jameson?"

"We have the agents' names, how to contact them and such, on a piece of paper hidden in the cabin somewhere," Rand said. "So this is how it goes. We take you out to the tree where the tape is stashed, tell you where that paper is, and you let us go. We leave, you come back and get the paper, and we all get what we want."

"What kind of trick are you pulling now?" Koslyn wanted to know, his expression wary.

"No tricks. We know we won't get away with crossing you a second time."

Koslyn took only a moment to mull the plan over. "Okay. You got a deal. The tape and that piece of paper for your lives." He motioned toward the front door with the barrel of his gun. "Get going. And remember that I'm still torn between the money and blowing you away, so don't try anything."

They stepped into the blackness of the forest, the rogue cop keeping a safe distance behind so he could cover them both. The crickets buzzed loudly around them. Nicole kept her arm around Rand, allowing her to whisper in his ear.

"What are we going to do now? The tape's back there."

"I found a great big hole out here the other night, an abandoned well or something. The boards covering it are so weak, I almost fell in and broke my neck. They'll never hold his weight. Just take a big step when I tell you to."

She nodded, holding him even tighter. "What if—"

"Stop whispering," Koslyn ordered. "It makes me nervous. How far is it to this tree of yours?"

"A little bit farther," Rand replied. He had to get Koslyn's mind off them. "How did you find us, anyway?"

The other man chuckled. "Good detective work. You keep forgetting what I am, Jameson. Once the goons let me go, I set to work checking you out. You're a pretty boring guy, you know that?"

"What did you expect? I'm just a businessman."

"I nosed around, found all kinds of people watching your homes, and figured you had gone to ground somewhere. One of your neighbors mentioned that you had a friend with a secluded mountain cabin. She even knew where it was, since you'd told her how to reach you when you went up there on vacation once."

"Mrs. Carlton," Rand grumbled. "I thought she liked me."

"It's amazing what people will tell a cop. But she seemed to have it in for you, something about cheating on your alimony."

Rand scowled. "Those creeps watching my house told her that. Now who'll water my plants when I'm gone?" He walked along muttering for a bit, then almost tripped when a horrible thought occurred to him. "Hey! Wait a minute. If she told you that, who else did she tell?"

"Us," a gruff voice announced from somewhere to their left. "Drop the gun, pal."

Koslyn crouched, scanning the trees. "What the—"

"I said drop it!"

Four men emerged from the trees, all dressed similarly in camouflage clothing. They all had automatic pistols in their hands, and they appeared quite anxious to use them.

"What is this?" Koslyn asked. "I'm an officer of the law, and you're interfering—"

One of the men pointed his pistol right at the middle of Koslyn's large stomach. "I'll interfere with a lot more than your duty if you don't drop that gun."

He dropped it. "Who are you guys?"

"These," Rand said, "are the rumor-spreading creeps."

"You four are disgusting," Nicole told them. "Telling lies, drinking and driving, not to mention going to that adult motel. Do your mothers know what you do for a living?"

One of the men chuckled. "This is going to be fun."

"I get her first."

"Shut up!" the one who appeared to be the leader yelled. "All of you." There were plenty of guns to go around. His was pointed at Rand. "The tape, Jameson. Now. It's all we want, and we're going to get it by any means you force us to use. Your decision."

This situation was way out of hand. Nicole was hugging Rand so tightly, he could barely breathe. And the truth of the matter was, he was fresh out of ideas.

"All right. All we want is this guy off our backs and to come out of this intact."

The leader shrugged. "Fine with me. The cop here might be a threat so he's history, in any case. You two don't mean a thing to us."

"Hey!" one of them objected. "The woman—"

"No time. The tape will buy you your pick of women."

"And if they talk?"

Another shrug from the leader. "Who cares?"

Rand hugged Nicole and sighed. "It's in the cabin."

"What?" Koslyn glared at him.

In the light of the moon filtering through the trees they could see the leader frown. "Then what were you doing out here?" he demanded.

"We were going to drop this big louse down a hole," Rand replied vindictively.

"Not a bad idea, at that," the man said. "Where is it?"

Rand pointed. There was still a chance. Perhaps in the confusion . . . "This way."

"I'll get you for this, Jameson."

"I sincerely doubt you'll be getting anyone ever again, cop. Now move."

With Rand and Nicole in front, Koslyn in the middle, and the four men bringing up the rear, they set off once again into the dappled black wall of the forest. They had barely taken more than a few steps, however, when a thunderous chatter erupted from the trees in front of them. A stream of bullets kicked up a cloud of dust at their feet.

"Freeze!" an electronically amplified voice commanded. "Everybody put your hands on your heads or we'll shred you like lettuce!" The submachine gun chattered again for emphasis.

Four pistols hit the ground. They all stood like statues, hands on their heads, as three well-dressed men stepped from behind the trees. One carried a bullhorn.

Nicole groaned. "What now?"

"It's the three feds who chased us in the blue sedan," Rand muttered. "What is this? A convention?"

"All right!" Koslyn shouted in relief. "Am I glad to see you guys. I was just about—"

"Shut up, Koslyn," one of the federal agents said curtly. "If we hadn't followed you up here

251

and these idiots hadn't intervened, I'm sure you would have gotten the tape and headed for the hills." He looked at one of the men with him. "Farley, cover them. Now, Sabine and Jameson."

Rand pointed back the way they had come. "It's in the cabin," he said resignedly. "I'll show you where it's hidden if you let Nicole and I get out of this loony operation."

The man rubbed his hands together. "Done. But a word of this to anyone and—"

"We know, we know," Nicole said, her shoulders sagging with fatigue at the insanity of it all. "You'll see to it our tax returns are audited from here to doomsday, right? Let's just get this over with."

The crowd tramped back through the forest to the cabin. At a curt order from the man with the machine gun they all stopped on the porch, the weather-beaten wood creaking beneath their combined weight.

"What is it, Farley?"

"I thought I heard something in there, sir."

"Such as?"

"Some sort of scratching, bumping noise, sir."

The head agent cleared his throat nervously and withdrew a revolver from a holster beneath his suit coat. "I'll go see," he announced.

"It's probably just raccoons," Rand assured him.

"Or that lunatic who goes around bashing into people with his truck, perhaps?" the man asked

252

haughtily. "We shall see." He cautiously slipped inside the cabin.

As the seconds ticked by, Farley, the man with the automatic weapon, got nervous. "Everything all right in there, sir?" he called out at last.

"Um, Farley, would you bring them all inside, please?"

He motioned with the weapon, and they all trooped through the door. The small living room practically overflowed with angry, disgruntled people. When they saw what awaited them, one or two gasps of surprise came from the group, as well as quite a few muttered epithets.

"Hello, Marsha," Rand said. "How nice to see you again, John."

Nicole closed her eyes for a moment, letting out a deep, exasperated sigh. "What a surprise. If I knew you all were coming, I would have gotten out the good china."

John had a gun to the dirty federal agent's head. Marsha was pointing hers at Farley. "Please drop the gun, Agent Farley, or my associate will be forced to ventilate your superior's skull."

"Do as she says, Farley!" the headman exclaimed.

Farley debated for a moment, quite obviously thinking of spraying the room with bullets. The crowd took a collective breath and held it, waiting for his decision. He put down the gun. Marsha immediately picked it up and handed it to

John, who took over covering the crowd. He, too, looked as if he might fire at any moment.

"Nice weapon, Farley," John said. "They must have raised the armament allowance over there."

Farley shrugged. "No, I bought it myself."

"Great," Nicole muttered. "Shoptalk."

"Everyone on the floor, please, facedown, arms and legs spread," Marsha requested. "Don't be silly, Rand. You and Nicole may use the chairs."

Carefully she went from man to man and checked them for weapons. She found a few, which she discarded out the open front door. Then she went and sat down at the kitchen table with Rand and Nicole. She smiled.

"Well. Isn't this cozy?"

"I'm getting a bit tired of asking this question," Rand said with disgust, "but how did you find us?"

Marsha laughed. "Oh, it was great fun. That was a naughty trick, putting the homing device on that police car. We were practically on top of them by the time we realized what was going on."

"They got suspicious and started following *us*," John said, grumbling. "We had to take a quick detour through a construction site to get away from them and ended up with three flat tires."

"Lucky in a way, though," Marsha continued. "While we were waiting for the flats to be fixed, we remembered we had another homing device hidden in the engine compartment of John's car.

It's remote-activated. Quite handy for when you forget where you park your car."

Nicole put her head down on her folded arms. "I've had it. I simply can't take any more of this. Tapes, spies, electronic gizmos, not to mention all these guns pointing at me." She turned her head and looked at Rand. "Can I throw up now?"

"Hold on for a bit and I'll join you," he replied, patting her on the back sympathetically. He looked at Marsha. "I didn't really plan to go through with the deal, you know. I'm no traitor."

"I suspected as much," she told him in an understanding tone. "We lied to you, too, though. We had no intention of buying it from you."

"To tell you the honest truth, I don't give a hoot anymore. Take the damn thing. Do whatever you like with it. All I want is to go back to a nice quiet life and marry Nicole."

Marsha chuckled. "Really? How nice," she said, grinning at Nicole. "Congratulations."

"It's still under discussion, actually," Nicole replied, raising her head and glaring at Rand disdainfully. "But we agree on one thing. Take the tape and leave us alone."

"You'll never get away with it, lady," Koslyn said, his voice muffled since he was still facedown on the floor.

"There's a lot of clout in this room," the leader of the federal team said in agreement. "You can't shoot us all. Your superiors wouldn't stand for it. Why don't we sit down and talk this over before you get in over your head?"

John laughed. "Tough talk coming from a man with his nose in the carpet."

"As a matter of fact," Marsha informed them, "we have been granted special dispensation in this case. John and I can pretty much do as we please with you all, so don't get any ideas about making a break for it."

"Special dispensation?" the federal man mumbled. "But only the—"

"Our orders come right from the top, yes," Marsha said, interrupting cheerfully. "Of course, we're going to bend the rules slightly. Providing none of you get out of hand, it is our intention to turn you over to the Justice Department. You three agents will fare better than the four mercenaries, and I imagine Lieutenant Koslyn's sentence will fall somewhere in between. But it's a whole lot better than being dead, don't you think?"

"Naturally the tape will be lost in a tragic fire that started when we captured you," John added. "Such a shame. But even that fits the bill. You see, we were to get the tape if possible and destroy it if not. The real prize in all this is you gentlemen, dirty tricksters brought to justice, with photographs and tapes of your deeds as evidence."

"We'll talk," Koslyn said threateningly. There was a general murmur of agreement from the others. "You'll go down too."

"Don't be silly," Marsha said, her disdain obvious. "You all know how the system works. Politically volatile situations like this are handled quickly and quietly. The package we'll hand them will be nice, neat, and expedient. We'll be the heroes, you'll be the scapegoats, and no one will listen to you because it would take too much time."

"Truth, justice, and the American way," Rand said bitterly. "I've had about as much of this as I can stomach."

Marsha nodded. "Quite understandable. The tape?"

"It's over there," Rand replied. "Behind a crack in the mantel over the fireplace." He watched, defeated and resigned to his loss, as she retrieved the tape from its hiding place. "You don't really have to burn down Jim's cabin, do you?"

"Afraid so." She shrugged sadly. "Your friend will be compensated for the loss, though. I'll leave you some forms to fill out."

"How kind of you," Nicole bit out.

Marsha turned to her partner. "Give me the gun, John, and I'll watch them while you set up the blaze."

"On the contrary, Marsha, my dear. You put *your* gun down and give me that tape."

Rand stared at him, dumbfounded. Nicole felt the hairs on the back of her neck stand up. Even the men on the floor risked turning their heads to look at the agent with the submachine gun. The weapon was now aimed at a point between them and Marsha. John had a horrible scowl on his face and an even nastier glint in his eyes.

In fact, the only one still smiling was Marsha. But it was a sad smile. "Care to tell me why?"

"Come off it, Marsha. You didn't really think I was taken in by your charade for an instant, did you? I knew the chief paired me with you because he thought I was dirty."

"It was suspected," Marsha admitted. "We arranged for some false codes to be sent through the Gladiola Connection, as a test of the system. Lo and behold, the codes showed up in Russian hands. There were a few other agents being watched, but you were our prime candidate."

John nodded. "I see. What would you have done if I had turned *you* in when you mentioned we should take the tape for ourselves?"

"Personally I would have been pleased, John," she replied. "You were a good agent once. It hit me hard when you agreed to the dirty deal. Why do you think I didn't blow the whistle on you right then and there?"

"Don't tell me you were giving me a chance to do the right thing and confess?" he asked derisively.

She sighed. "I was hoping you would. Or that maybe you were just going along with me to catch *me* in the act." Slowly and deliberately she put her gun down on the kitchen table and moved away from it. "Obviously I have had better ideas. What are you going to do now? It was all a setup, you know. There's no way you can get away with it now."

"I still have the tape," he said, stepping carefully over to her and grabbing it. "And I know it's real."

Marsha nodded. "It had to be. We couldn't have anyone figuring out what we were up to. The dirty agent had to rise to the bait so we could stop this leak once and for all."

"Too bad it didn't work out. Too bad for you, that is. You shouldn't have given me this chance, Marsha. There's a spot waiting for me on the KGB. They'll see to it I get away with this," he said, holding up the tape like a trophy. "And all your subterfuge has gotten you is a massacre. I'll have to kill you all."

Nicole couldn't stand it. "Time out!" she yelled, standing up and waving her arms. "I don't understand any of this! Will one of you please tell me what's going on?"

"Nicole!" Rand said urgently, pulling her back into her seat. "I don't think now is quite the time to ask for explanations."

"Why not?" Tears of anger and frustration were trickling down her face. "You heard him. He's going to kill us all."

Marsha looked at John. He nodded, so she gave Nicole a comforting pat on the back and said, "It's really quite simple, Nicole, although you certainly have every reason to be confused. There are only two people in this room who knew what was going on from the very beginning, knew all about the scheme to trap John, knew I was using you both toward that end, and were, as Rand put it, good guys."

"Two?" Nicole queried. "But—"

"Me for one. I'm good as gold." She picked up her gun and pointed it at John. "And then there's Agent Farley over there. The one with the .44 Magnum revolver aimed at John's masculinity," she said. "Do raise your sights a bit, Farley. Aim for something larger."

John's eyes seemed to bulge as he spun to find Marsha's statement to be true. His face a mask of hatred, he readied the submachine gun for firing. "Go ahead and shoot! I can take you all with me before I go down!"

He pulled the trigger. There was a loud click, then silence. Marsha's throaty chuckle broke the horrified spell that had fallen over the onlookers.

"You don't really think I'd give a loaded gun to a suspected traitor, do you, John?"

"Damn you!" he cried, throwing the weapon on the floor.

"Hey!" Farley objected. "That's my gun, chum, and it works fine when it has a real clip in it." In a fluid motion he scooped the weapon off the floor, ejected the blank magazine, and inserted a full one. "Which you'll find out firsthand if you move a muscle," he said, getting to his feet and backing into one corner of the room. "That goes for all you bums."

Marsha let out a long, heavy sigh. "Lord, it feels good almost to be done with this mess.

Rand, would you mind going out to my car and radioing for backup?"

"My pleasure. Come on, Nicole," he said, helping her to her feet. "You can show me how."

"Come on, feet," Nicole said, feeling shaky from all the excitement. "You can do it."

"Just punch the button and say 'Gladiola.' There's someone listening. Farley, let's get these guys handcuffed. I hope I brought enough. I—" She stopped, her head cocked to one side. "What was that noise?"

"Squirrels," Rand said knowingly.

Nicole laughed. It felt wonderful to be alive. "No, I'll bet it's raccoons."

"There it is again!" Marsha exclaimed.

It was an odd noise, like someone—or something—panting. And it was getting closer. Suddenly an eerie howl split the night. The sound of movement on the porch made all eyes turn toward the open front door. A long, indistinct shadow spilled into the room as whatever it was approached the threshold.

Then they saw it. Outlined by the moon, a horrendous, furry shape appeared in the doorway. It seemed at least seven feet tall, with gray fur covering its body from fuzzy head to sharp-clawed paws. Golden eyes gleamed at them. Fangs like razors glistened in the light.

"A giant wolf!" Nicole screamed, and promptly fainted.

Rand caught her. "Hello, Jim. Join the party."

The beast stepped into the room, its paws on its hips. "What the heck is going on here? And who's going to pay for the mess all those cars made out of my wildflowers?"

CHAPTER FOURTEEN

Rand strode across the Sabine grounds, heading for the office. Enough was enough. Nicole had asked him for some time to think, and he had given it to her, the worst six days of his life. But he was through waiting. Whatever her answer, he wanted it now, face-to-face, the same way this whole thing had started.

"Hey! Give me a hand over here, will you?"

"What?" Looking around impatiently, Rand saw a broad-shouldered man working on a delivery van near the loading dock. "Me?" he asked.

"You'll do. I need some help with this engine."

As Rand approached, he saw that the man was struggling with something under the hood of the van. He was older than Rand, with a full head of salt-and-pepper hair, the muscular arms displayed by the rolled-up sleeves of his mechanic's overalls deeply tanned.

"What's the problem?" Rand inquired.

"Hand me that wrench there, will you?" His voice was deep and gruff. "I've got hold of this nut under here and can't let go or it'll drop into the cowling and disappear."

Rand handed him the wrench. "Are you the Sabine mechanic?"

The man laughed heartily. "Mechanic, irrigation expert, cooling-fan repairman, you name it, I do it around here." His tongue worried the corner of his mouth as he concentrated on his task. "Hold that hose out of my way, will you? I can't see a thing."

"Sure." Rand peered at the man. "You look kind of familiar." He must have seen him on the tour Nicole gave him that first day they met.

The man glanced at Rand. "So do you." He returned to his task. "Watch that valve cover. It's all greasy."

"No problem."

"Good to see a man who isn't afraid to get his hands dirty these days."

Rand chuckled. "I know what you mean. I have to work on my own delivery vans most of the time too."

"Are you in the flower trade?"

"Sure am. The name's Rand. Rand Jameson."

As he thought, the name registered. The man jerked his head and hit it on the hood. "Ouch! Well, I'll be. Jameson."

"Still want my help?" Rand asked. "I understand I'm not too well liked around here."

He shrugged. "They'll get over it."

"I'm here to see your boss, actually," Rand

told him, frowning at his comment. "Is she here today?"

"My boss," the man replied, "is at home fussing over the big dinner she's planned for this evening. She always throws one of these things the Friday we get back from our annual vacation. As a matter of fact, I believe you're invited, Rand." He chuckled. "Or so the boss tells me."

Rand closed his eyes. "Your name is . . ."

"Sabine. Richard Sabine, Nicole's father."

"Oh, Lord," Rand muttered.

Richard Sabine straightened and eased his head out of the van's engine compartment. He slapped the big wrench in his hand against the palm of his other hand, gazing at Rand thoughtfully. He took a step toward the younger man.

"I believe you and I have some talking to do, Rand."

"I—"

"There has been quite a bit of gossip going around about what happened while my wife and I were gone," Nicole's father continued. "I guess you and my daughter had quite an adventure. On the run, hiding out together." Slap went the wrench against his palm. "Yes, I'd say we have a lot of talking to do."

Rand swallowed heavily as the big man advanced upon him. "Let me explain. Nicole and I—"

"Her sister, Jean, tells me you even had some kind of thing going for each other by the time the intrigue was over." Slap, slap. "Is that right?"

"Mr. Sabine," Rand said hurriedly, "may I take this opportunity to respectfully ask for your daughter's hand in marriage?"

Richard stopped in his tracks. He glared at Rand for a moment, then burst out laughing. "Well, you can ask," he replied with a wide grin, "but—"

"We love each other, sir. I asked her a week ago, but she said she wanted some time to think it over."

He nodded. "I know. I also know she hasn't been much use around here all week. Nicole's a thinker, you see, always has been," Richard informed him. "Are you a thinker, Rand?"

"I think it's about time she and I discussed our plans face-to-face," Rand replied, instantly more at ease when her father put down the wrench and wiped his hands on a rag. "I realize there are a lot of things to consider. She's a major part of your business—"

"Indispensable," Richard agreed.

Rand nodded. "Yes. But I love her, and if she feels the same about me, I'm going to marry her. I figure the rest we can work out together—as a family, so to speak."

"I agree. Like I said, we have some talking to do. You'll come to dinner this evening."

It wasn't a request. "Of course."

"Now, about your proposal," Richard added. "You have to understand the way things work around here. There is a chain of command. Tradition, you know. Before you can ask Nicole, you have to ask me, and before you can ask me, you have to ask my father."

Rand wasn't thrilled by the prospect but somehow had known it would be this way. "Vin? I have to ask Vin if I can ask you if I can ask Nicole to marry me?"

"Confusing, isn't it?" Richard slapped Rand on the back. Years of running a flower-growing operation had made him quite strong. "You'll get the hang of it, though. All part of being a Sabine, which, whether you know it yet or not, is exactly what you'll be if you marry into this family, no matter what name you were born with."

"I sort of figured that would be the case," Rand admitted with a resolute grin.

"Vin's in his hothouse." He extended his hand. "See you tonight, Rand. And good luck."

Rand shook his head. "Thanks. I have the feeling I'll need it," he muttered as he went in search of the Sabine patriarch.

Vin scarcely looked up when Rand entered the hothouse. He was tending his orchids, a bizarre, pungent mixture of liquid fertilizer in a bucket on one side of him, a glass of white wine close at hand on the other.

"Hello, Toadstool."

Rand sighed. "Vin. How are you this fine afternoon?"

"Good. The sun is warm, the soil is rich, my orchids have survived the thrips." He lifted the glass of wine and took a swallow. "And I have convinced my aches and pains to leave me alone today. You?"

"Fine," Rand lied.

"You are looking for Nicole?"

"I will be in a little while. Right now I need to speak with you."

Vin finally turned and looked at the younger man. His bushy eyebrows shot up questioningly. "So?" He straightened and went to a table that had been strategically placed in the shade, taking a seat and waving his hand for Rand to do the same. "Hand me my glass, please. There's another over there, if you care to join me."

"I would, thanks."

After retrieving the glasses Rand sat down on the other side of the small table. Vin poured him some wine. They sipped it in silence for a moment, Rand slowly getting used to the heat and humidity while the Sabine patriarch enjoyed the beauty of his exotic orchids.

"You'll have to talk louder than that, Toadstool," Vin said. "My ears aren't what they used to be."

Rand chuckled. "I haven't said anything yet, Vin. By the way, I don't suppose I could convince you to call me Rand?"

He shrugged. "Anything is possible. Nicole tells me you have been very busy this past week. Not having a family to run things in your absence, I suppose your business suffered from this incident with the tape?"

"To a degree," Rand replied. "I have good people working for me. They managed to muddle through."

"Then why has it taken you so long to come see me?" Vin inquired, studying his wineglass.

"You've been expecting me?"

Vin squinted at him. "Is it your habit, young man, to answer a question with a question?"

"I've stayed away at Nicole's request," Rand explained. "She said she needed time to think."

"Hmm," Vin said thoughtfully. "She has done plenty of that, wandering around the greenhouses, sitting in her office staring into space."

"Vin—"

"Do you know anything about the propagation of orchids, Toadstool?" he said, interrupting.

"Excuse me?"

"It's quite a task," Vin continued, as if Rand hadn't spoken. "The seed is so fine, it looks like a coarse powder. To germinate it one must spread it upon a sterilized jelly made of balanced nutrients, contained in a flask that must be kept warm at all times. In this carefully controlled environment a mere pinch can provide thousands of potential seedlings. When the shoots reach the proper size, they are removed from the flask and placed in rich soil to grow."

Rand frowned. "That's fascinating, but—"

"Such a process!" Vin exclaimed. "It always amazes me when they start to bloom, a flower of such tender beauty from a seed so small." He poured them both more wine. "And yet, there they are, growing all around us. We must savor things such as this in our lives, don't you think?"

"Yes, Vin," Rand answered dutifully.

He nodded in satisfaction. "I have been a grower all my life. I know when something is alive and sprouting. Do you believe this, Toadstool?"

"Yes, Vin."

"And do you know what to do with something that is sprouting, young man?" Vin asked, looking at Rand intently.

Rand smiled at him. "You nurture it."

"That is correct. If you leave it alone, it will wither and die. Am I getting through to you?"

There was more to this conversation than seedlings and good gardening methods. "I think so," Rand replied.

"Bah!" Vin exclaimed, rising from his chair. "Thinking. There has been entirely too much thinking going on around here. If you expect anything to grow, you're going to have to get your hands dirty."

Rand got up too. "Thanks, Vin."

The older man extended his hand. Rand took it, astounded by the strength of his grip. "I love that sprout, Rand," Vincent Sabine said.

"So do I, Vin."

"Then go find her! *Vite!*"

Nicole strolled among the carnations, lost in thought. So many things to consider, but her mind seemed to shrug off every attempt to view them with any logic. All she could think of was Rand and the way they had parted a week ago.

Things were slowly returning to normal. Her apartment had been cleaned and straightened, and the paperwork to authorize reimbursement for the destroyed flower shipment was grinding through the government gears. As the days slipped by, however, Nicole had come to realize that the meaning of normal had changed for her.

Normal was being with Rand, talking to him, laughing with him, even fighting with him. Normal was falling asleep in his arms. There was no returning to the way things had been before, because her view of life had completely changed. The only kind of competition she wanted to enter into with Rand now was one of the most sensual kind.

She loved him. There wasn't a doubt in her mind now. He loved her, too, enough that he had allowed her this time to herself. He hadn't been happy about it, of course, and the desperation in his eyes as she had left him haunted her. But couldn't he see how difficult it would be?

"Some water, I think."

Nicole whirled around at the sound of his voice. "Rand!" she cried. "What did you say?"

"Water. A pinch of fertilizer. And," he added sternly, though his heart was soaring among the clouds, "I think it's high time I planted your roots firmly in the earth."

He swept her into his arms and kissed her. She felt so good, he wanted to devour her, his tongue probing the sweet cavern of her mouth, his lips tasting hers until she gasped for breath.

"I've missed you, Nicole. I never want to be parted from you again."

"I missed you too. I wanted time to think, but I couldn't think of anything but you. What were you talking about a moment ago?" she murmured, her face buried against his throat as she held him close.

"I have been instructed to nurture you," he replied, pulling back to look into her eyes. "And nurture you I shall. I believe you owe me an answer to a certain question I asked you a week ago."

Nicole went limp in his arms as she looked into those warm, loving hazel eyes. "Oh, Rand. I love you. I want to marry you and have your children. And it would be fantastic if they grew up in this business. But do you know what this means?" she asked, worry gripping her heart again. "A merger between Sabine and Jameson!"

"I was thinking more along the lines of a big church wedding myself," he remarked. "And merger may be too organized a word for what we'll have, in any case. But what's wrong with a partnership of sorts?"

"Vin will simply explode!"

"Well, then," Rand said, laughing softly and kissing the tip of her nose, "we'll just have to take defensive action. We'll keep him soused until our first child is born."

"Hmm." She seriously considered it. "No, that wouldn't work. We'd be broke in a week."

"I was joking, dear. I just left him. Who do you think told me to nurture you?"

"Vin said that?" she asked, eyes wide with surprise.

"He also," Rand informed her proudly, "shook my hand and called me by my first name."

"Vin?"

"As did your father."

Nicole grasped at his collar dramatically. "Hold me close. I may faint."

"I'll hold you close no matter what." He kissed her again, hugging her tightly. "You're bound to me now, Nicole, by your own traditions. I'll never let you go."

"I'll never want you to," she vowed.

"By the way, I'm coming to dinner tonight, undoubtedly to be initiated into the Sabine clan," he said uneasily. "Will it hurt?"

"Oh, my," Nicole murmured. "That depends: Have you ever taken a blood oath before?"

It turned out to be quite a dinner. The Sabines and their employees, Rand and his employees, as well as the woman who was still calling herself Marsha, all enjoying the hospitality of Nicole's mother and father like one big, happy family. The gathering was so large, it spilled out of the Sabine home and across the backyard, even gathering in a few neighbors along the way.

This was, after all, an auspicious occasion.

273

There was to be a marriage. There was also to be a sort of convoluted partnership and merger between the Sabine and Jameson businesses. Everyone was excited, and just about everyone of age was slightly tipsy.

"He has a mole shaped like a rabbit on his—"

"That'll be enough of that!" Rand exclaimed, deciding it was about time to interrupt the secretive conversation between Marsha and his wife-to-be. "I'll not have you spreading rumors."

Nicole patted Rand on his very masculine rear end. "It's not a rumor, dear. It's a fact."

"Besides, the whole world knows, Rand," Marsha told him. "Or at least a select portion of the world. You remember that tape you made of Koslyn?"

Rand's mouth dropped open. He looked at Nicole in outrage. "You were supposed to have erased that part!"

"Oops!" Nicole shrugged innocently. "Sorry."

"I'll just bet you are."

Nicole decided to change the subject. "So. I thought you were over there with my Dad and Vin, congratulating each other on working out a deal."

"I got lonely," he said, slipping his arm around her waist. He looked at Marsha. "How goes the spy trade?"

She shrugged. "They win some, we win some. By the way, I have something for you two." She reached out and shook his hand, then Nicole's.

"There you go. Straight from the president to you."

"That's it?" Rand asked, looking at his hand.

"No brass band?" Nicole queried. "No plaque to hang on the wall thanking us for our patriotism and courage under fire?"

"Sorry. I'm afraid you'll have to remain silent heroes. The tape finally got where it was intended to go, the intelligence community and one local police precinct are a bit cleaner these days, and for obvious reasons I must ask you to keep quiet about everything that happened." She grinned. "I'm sure two such upstanding citizens can do that, can't they? Otherwise . . ."

"Our lips are sealed," Nicole said quickly.

"To each other," Rand agreed, dipping his head to give her a kiss. "We've had enough intrigue for a lifetime."

Marsha raised her eyebrows. "Oh, you never know," she said cryptically. "Well, I have to run. Thank your beautiful mother for all the food, Nicole."

"Will do. You'll come to the wedding, won't you?"

"If I can. Bye!"

They watched her leave, arms around each other, love in the air around them like the perfume of a thousand flowers. It didn't bother either of them that a handshake was all they had gotten for the ordeal they had endured.

Rand and Nicole had managed to gain a prize

much more valuable than any official commendation. A very special delivery had been made straight to their hearts, a bouquet of love, and it would be them against the world from now on.

Rand dropped the pen he was holding on a stack of invoices when she entered his small, windowless office. "Nicole, what's wrong?"

Her face was clouded with worry as she looked at him. "I heard you and Dad arguing earlier today."

Even now, seven months after their marriage, Nicole still feared that everything wasn't going to work out in the long run between her family and him. Though they had willingly agreed to the merger in theory, putting it into day-to-day practice had its problems.

Rand smiled at her, relieved by her answer. "Don't forget Vin. He was in on that argument too." The crusty old man had become a very close friend and adviser to him, never hesitating to give his opinion, solicited or not. "Yelling louder than everyone else, I might add."

"What's wrong now?"

"Nothing much. We had a minor disagreement over the new computerized watering system for the greenhouses, that's all," Rand told her. "As usual, Vin is taking the view that technology and flowers don't mix."

Sabine and Jameson had merged their businesses on Sabine land. Rand was completely in charge of importing and brokering cut flowers for both companies, having consolidated them into one solid unit. And no one—with the exception of his wife, naturally—was allowed to question his decisions. Rand knew their increased profits proved his expertise.

His intrusion into the growing area, however, was another matter entirely. Nicole collapsed in a chair in front of his new oak desk and closed her eyes.

"You call that minor, with all that shouting?"

Rand shrugged. "We always shout. Vin says it helps keep one's juices flowing," he told her, enjoying the sight of her firm breasts jutting against her blouse. "And I'm inclined to believe him."

Nicole sighed. It was all her fault. She now helped her father run the grower side and was directing Sabine toward specializing in growing certain hard-to-get products. It was where she wanted to be, with her hands in the soil half the time and her mind on renewed growth of their business the rest of the time.

As the liaison between the two operations, she had planned on informing the family of the new watering system herself but had to admit that she'd been stalling, waiting for just the right moment, not wanting to upset anyone with yet another change.

"Who told them?"

"The company installing the system," Rand told her dryly, chuckling quietly as his mind flashed on an image of the startled faces of the workers when the arguing began. The Sabine family took some getting used to; no one was afraid to add their opinion to any discussion. "They arrived to start the job."

"Oh, no!" It had completely slipped her mind that they were coming today. And now it was her responsibility to make peace in the family one more time. The new system was her department, even if it had been Rand's idea originally. "I'll go talk to them."

"It's been settled."

Her eyes flashed open, and she stared at her husband. "What? How?" Nicole demanded.

"I simply told them that I seduced you into agreeing with me on this."

Nicole jumped out of her chair, her face turning a very becoming pink. "You didn't!"

"And they believed me too." Rand leaned back in his swivel chair and crossed his arms behind his head.

"Rand Jameson! How could you?"

"Easily, Nicole Jameson!"

"This is a business!"

"Yes, it is, Nicole," he agreed, getting out of his chair and walking over to her. He gently enfolded her in his embrace, resting his head on top of her silky blond hair. "A family business. And you have got to stop trying to run interference between me and the entire Sabine clan."

Nicole looked up at him, trying to ignore the way her body was reacting to his. "But . . ."

"Ssh," he whispered, placing his index finger on her petal-soft lips. "You're tearing yourself apart because of this divided loyalty you feel. Let it be."

"But I do it—"

He finished the sentence for her. "Because you love all of us. We know that, darling."

Nicole pulled away from him. "You don't understand!"

Rand followed her with his eyes, enjoying the way her body moved as she paced around the small office. At last he had walls and privacy. It was giving him ideas.

"I understand more than you think I do, Nicole. You've got to accept things as they're going to be from now on."

She sat wearily on the edge of his desk. "What?"

"Darling, I'm fully capable of fighting all my own battles in this business, and I intend to do so in the future. It was my mistake to let you try to keep the peace between everyone."

"Someone has to!"

Rand leaned back against the closed office door and crossed his arms over his chest. "No, they don't. From now on it's every man or woman for themselves."

"But the arguments!" The few blazing verbal

fights had at times been enough to start forest fires.

"There was always a lot of opposition to any changes you made or implemented before marrying me, remember."

Nicole thought back. "Well, yes, but—"

"Then things haven't changed that much. Now everyone vents their frustrations on me instead of you, and I don't mind. You've got to modernize to stay competitive, or you're going to be out of the growing business."

"I know. I've always known. But does efficiency always have to come about as the result of a yelling match?"

"We're not really arguing most of the time. I like discussing things with your family, especially with your father and Vin, very vocally over a bottle of good wine—though it can get mind-boggling at times," he admitted. He was at a distinct disadvantage when they flew off into French, but he was working on that. "I'm learning so much from them, not just about business but also about every facet of life. They enjoy it, too, immensely, even if we don't agree ninety percent of the time."

Nicole was aware that her entire family was emotional, even volatile at times, and passionately outspoken toward what they believed in. And they did relish a good discussion. Deep inside she knew that Rand was right, and the implications of what he said were a welcome relief.

Rand watched her, knowing the battle over her

family loyalty wasn't finished. But he'd made his decision with Vin's help. Time. Vin had emphasized that. Don't rush her. Give her time to accept and like the changes, to let someone else shoulder part of the responsibility just as you do when you move or transplant growing flowers. Nurture them carefully and they will respond to your ways.

"You know what I'd really like?" Rand asked her softly, loudly clicking the dead-bolt lock behind him. "I'd like that passionate body of yours on top of mine."

Nicole slid off the desk and moved cautiously back. "Now, Rand," she murmured, her own voice low and soft. All of her senses were suddenly tingling with anticipation, her body ready and eager for his. They were in their busy season right now and never seemed to have as much time for each other as they wanted. "We can't. Can we?"

"We're the bosses, remember?" he whispered, reaching out and pulling her toward him, enfolding her in his captive embrace. "We can do anything we want."

She tilted her head back, avoiding the sensuous feel of his lips on hers. "But we're at work!" she protested weakly, running her fingers through his coal-black hair.

"So we'll work on this," he murmured, dropping the pins from her hair one by one. Her blond tresses came tumbling down, and he inhaled the sweet scent, burying his face in the soft, downy texture. "I love you, Nicole."

"And I love you. But . . ." Nicole wanted to give in, but reality kept surfacing its ugly head in her mind. "Rand, darling, don't you have an appointment this afternoon?"

"So I'll work fast," he returned, removing her blouse.

"I—I . . . oh, what the heck." She moaned softly as his hands skimmed over her skin, touching, teasing, arousing her wildly.

"Let the world wait. Sometimes we have to put ourselves first, like now," he whispered, drawing her down onto the couch.

Nicole flowed with him, entering his waiting embrace eagerly. This was where she belonged, in the arms of the man she loved. In his arms she left the troubled world behind, seeking, finding, and giving joy.

They came together eagerly, clothing in disarray, their desire for each other bubbling out of control. The sweetness of this stolen moment filled them with one breathless sensation after another. Feeling deliciously wicked, they laughed together as they shared the shuddering culmination of their love, clasped tightly in each other's arms.

Rand smoothed the damp, silky blond hair away from her face. "I love you," he whispered softly.

"Mmm," Nicole murmured, nuzzling the

strong column of his throat, burying her face in its warmth, completely relaxed. "I love you too."

His hands roved over her, settling on her gently rounded stomach. "When are you going to tell the family?"

"Soon," she promised, liking the almost reverent way his fingers traced the swelling curve of her belly. He kissed her there, his eyes bright with the awareness of the new life growing within her.

"You're beginning to show," he teased, drawing exaggerated curves over her once flat stomach.

"Not that much," she returned, pressing his hands back to her skin. "They'll just think I'm getting fat with contentment. The Sabine heritage."

"These," he murmured wickedly, cupping her already full breasts, "will give you away. I swear they grow each day."

"And you like that?"

"I like the thought of every part of you growing with our child inside you." Rand cradled her face between his hands. "You're like an exotic lily bud that's slowly begun to open. Each day a little more of your inner beauty will reveal itself to me."

Nicole was deeply touched by the depth of his feelings for her, just as strong as her feelings for him. Her eyes shimmered with unshed tears. The danger they had faced together seemed years away now, leaving only the certain knowledge that as long as they were together, no problem was insurmountable.

"Hey, don't cry, love," he whispered, brushing a single tear from the corner of her eye with his thumb.

"They're tears of joy, Rand," she whispered, smoothing the frown from his face.

"Are you sure?"

"Yes, I'm very sure."

A discreet knock penetrated their haven. "Shh!" Nicole said, covering his mouth with her hand. "Maybe they'll go away."

"Everyone knows we're in here."

"So let their imaginations run wild," she returned, rolling on top of him. "I'm not done with you yet."

"I'm all yours."

"Forever?" she asked, hugging him fiercely.

"Forever."